the

BLOODBATH

BACHELORETTE

a black comedy

DOK & JAN

BLOODBATH BACHELORETTE

ISBN: 979-8-9930266-0-2

Published by DOK Publishing

For inquiries, please email info@dokproductions.com

🎉 The Itinerary 🎉

WEDNESDAY:
Arrival & Vibes

Best Wednesday Looks 🍱 Hibachi Dinner

THURSDAY:
Neon Thirst Trap Thursday

👙 Neon Fits + Brunch 🏖️ Pool Party 🕺 Club Night

FRIDAY:
Naughty & Nautical

🛥️ Yacht Party 🖤 **Black Out Club Night!**

SATURDAY:
Sexy Safari

🐆 Animal Print Pole Class 🐚 Beach Concert

SUNDAY:
Recovery

💆 Spa Recovery Day 🌙 Secret Night Adventure

TULUM INCIDENT REPORT

Filed by: Det. J. Ramirez

Subject: Bachelorette Trip Fatalities / Cartel Involvement

Date: [REDACTED]

Summary: Thirteen American tourists (11 female, 2 male) traveled to Tulum for a bachelorette party. The trip quickly unraveled into a series of fatal incidents, suspected foul play, and cartel entanglement.

Preliminary Timeline:

Arrival: Severe turbulence on the flight. Group reportedly witnessed a cartel shootout at the bus depot.

At the Resort: A string of suspicious deaths followed. Names have been redacted to protect identity until families are notified:

- **NAME REDACTED** – Jet ski explosion

- **NAME REDACTED** – Lost at sea

- **NAME REDACTED** – Drowned

- **NAME REDACTED** – Sauna fire

- **NAME REDACTED** – Golf cart crash

- **NAME REDACTED** – Electrocution

-

-

- **NAME REDACTED** – Hit by cartel vehicle

- **NAME REDACTED** – Missing
     (presumed deceased)

Note: Local coroner ran out of emesis bags. Resupply pending.

Ongoing Investigation: Conflicting reports surround Liv (maid of honor) and "Sanguine Rose" (alleged drug supplier). Both went missing in the jungle and were possibly mistaken for federal agents. Sources claim they briefly led a cartel while under the influence of narcotics. They returned shortly before this filing—barefoot, disoriented, and wearing cartel gold chains.

Status: U.S. and Mexican authorities are processing the scene. Victim IDs ongoing. Surveillance and social media are being reviewed under the casefile:

Bloodbath Bachelorette

I

FREAKY FLIGHT DAY

You can start reading here if you have the attention span to do so and finish right about here if you don't. You might have already tossed this unread book onto your nightstand to rot while you rot away doomscrolling. Or if reading is not your thing, and this story gets made into a movie then by Christ, you can just see it in a theatre while getting jerked off or fingerbanged by your local slut. Or maybe just wait a few weeks and stream it on TV while you wank one out in the comfort and privacy of your own home. The latter is how Liv would prefer it. Her long-term boyfriend just dumped her ass. Sometimes jerking off is better. Masturbation rarely leads to heartache.

So fast forward and fresh from her doctor's office, Liv boarded her flight to Tulum, Mexico to attend the bachelorette party of one of her oldest and bestest friends who we shall refer to in this story as "the Bride." Does the Bride have a name? Yes, of course she does. But is her name important? Absolutely not and why would it be? Because you have met the Bride before. Probably not exactly her but a bitch or asshole or jerk just like her. They come in all shapes, forms, sizes, sexes and genders. You might have even seen them on the news. They are the hyper narcissist, the zero self-awareness, the kind of creature who thinks the world revolves around them. The one who thinks their shit don't stink when they're the one who forgot to flush.

A few in-flight cocktails and in-flight movies later our hapless protagonist Liv looked up from her seat at 23C to the

Bride seated at 23A. The Bride was hot pink and pastel, sparkling and bedazzled with a tiara and veil. It screamed: "Look at me!" Liv was in stark contrast, black on black, a shirt she had worn to bed the night before, sweaty. The two's faces glowed blue and yellow with the light of their in-flight entertainment screens. Wedged between the two was a passed out Drunk Slob slumped over like a dead fish out of water, and he smelled as much. The plane bumped up and down and a toddler screamed for his mommy.

"Ladies and gentlemen, this is your captain speaking," was heard over the PA. "We have begun our initial descent into Tulum."

"Finally," The Bride slurred and took a sloppy shot of her tequila soda, lipstick on the rim, drink running down her stubbled cheek. "Get me the fuck off this plane and into a pool. Liv, I need another drink. You?"

"I'm good." Liv rubbed her sore abdomen. Her pain was growing.

"You okay?" The Bride asked. "You've been moaning this whole flight." The Bride looked up and down the aisle for a flight attendant.

"I'm good, just cramping real bad is all."

"Sheesh, then take a fucking Midol and wash it down with some tequila." The Bride chewed on some more ice and the captain came back on over the PA.

"If you could please place your seatbacks and tray tables to their upright position, we'll be landing shortly." He said over static. The plane rumbled and jostled again to the moans of drunk and pissed off passengers. Liv raised her tray table and locked it in place and SNAP the lock snapped off broken. What luck.

"Shit." She sighed in disbelief.

"Wow Liv." The Bride chortled, which is a really ugly word for an ugly laugh for an ugly person. Liv worked in vain to get that tray table back up but it was no use.

"Figures with my luck."

"Don't say that!" The Bride spat into her old drink. "As my maid of honor, it's your job-" The Bride stopped short when the Drunk Slob slumped over and dropped his heavy head on her shoulder.

"Ew!" The Bride gave the Drunk a hefty shove. He stirred and fell onto Liv's tray table as the plane jumped up and down. The fasten seatbelt sign turned on.

"Ladies and gentlemen as you see I have turned on the fasten seatbelt sign." The captain spoke again. "We're expecting a few bumps on the descent, nothing major. The seatbelt sign is on so please buckle up, sit back, relax and enjoy the flight."

"As I was saying." The Bride continued undeterred as Liv nudged the Drunk Slob upright as gracefully as one can who was just drooled on. "As I was saying it's your job to set the mood for MY party. Positive vibes only, Liv!"

"I know, I know," Liv regained her composure. "I just don't know any of your friends."

"They're not just my friends... they are my sorority sisters! You'll love them! They don't bite. They are absolutely harmless. I've told them all about you." The Bride looked back and waved to two of her Delta Sorority sisters sat two rows back. They were the fashionable blondes Heather and Meadow.

If you squinted your eyes and tilted your head you might mistake the two for blonde wig-wearing Burt and Ernie from Sesame Street. A flight attendant walked down the aisle. "You know what Liv, let's get you a drink. Stewardess!"

"I'm good." Liv said.

"What, are you pregnant or something?" The Bride joked.

"No." Liv answered nervously.

"God I would hope not." The Bride waved at the flight attendant and the Drunk Slob slumped down again, falling onto Liv's shoulder.

"Ma'am, if you could please raise and lock your tray table. We are landing." The flight attendant asked Liv. "Thank you."

"No problem, sorry." Liv pushed the Drunk off of her as politely as one could who was just drooled on for the second time and she lifted up the tray table.

"Hi yes." The Bride grabbed the flight attendant's attention. "Can I get another tequila soda? Better make it a double. And the same for my maid of honor here." The flight attendant rolled her eyes and made her way down the aisle making sure passengers were prepped for landing. The pissed off Bride unbuckled her seatbelt and stood up. "Fine! I'll get it myself."

"The seatbelt sign is on." Liv reminded her pointing. "We should really stay seated."

"Oh Liv, what are you 10 years old? The seatbelt sign is such a joke!" The Bride tried and failed at flagging down another flight attendant, then huffed and puffed and held her arms up in defeat to Heather and Meadow. "What does a Bride to be need to do to get a drink around here?" She said loud enough to make a scene. Heather held up three tequila nips tucked between her pudgy pink painted fingers.

"Get over here girly!" Meadow shouted waving to the Bride to be.

"Sit with us!" Blonde bimbo Heather called out.

"Excuse me!" The Bride jostled the Drunk Slob awake. "I need to get to my friends. Move!" The Drunk grunted and shifted his big fat stomach letting the Bride through. The Drunk leaned in at the optimal moment as the Bride's breasts rubbed across his face. "Pervert!" She hissed hopping over him and nearly tripping over Liv's broken tray table. She collected herself and looked up to her oldest friend. "I'll be right back." She sing-songed and slid down the aisle on her way to her sorority sisters. A sweet old lady was sat in the aisle seat beside Meadow and Heather.

"Excuse me miss." Meadow asked her. "Would you mind switching seats with our friend here? She's getting married!"

"I don't think we should be up," The old woman said gently.

"It's fine," the Bride insisted. "Look at me—I'm up!"

"Come on, it's her bachelorette party! You must!" Heather kept on.

"Passengers," A flight attendant spoke firmly through a PA system. "We remind you to take your seats immediately."

"Come on!" The Bride nudged the old lady. "My seat is closer to the front anyway, and it's a window seat so you get the view when we land! It's an upgrade!"

"Ma'am" The flight attendant was there, eyes like laser beams. She spoke firmly to the bride. "Return to your seat immediately."

"Hi yes, can I get another tequila soda, a double, and the same for my friends. This sweet old lady here offered to switch seats with me." The Bride lied to the flight attendant.

"I did?" The old woman asked confused.

"Yes, remember? You're getting an upgrade by moving to seat 23A. It's window!" Lied Meadow but the flight attendant shook her head no.

"You can't just change seats mid-flight." The flight attendant clenched her jaw. "It's against the rules and the seatbelt sign is on." Just then the seatbelt sign dinged off.

"See?" The Bride said ugly smugly. The sweet old lady unbuckled her seatbelt and rose out of her seat with a crack in her back.

"It's fine." She said to the flight attendant. "She can have my seat. It's good to be with friends."

"Alright, but quickly please ma'am we must take our seats." Said the flight attendant. "I'll escort you."

"Congratulations to you!" The sweet old lady said to the Bride as she was escorted up the aisle. The Bride landed triumphantly in her new seat.

"Three tequila sodas please. Double!"

"With Lime!" Meadow shouted.

"Oh my god what is that smell?"

"It's that old lady!"

"Gross."

Meanwhile Liv slid into the window seat squeezing past the snoring slob. She winced, her cramping worse than ever. Heather and Meadow snickered and gossiped with the bride, something Liv didn't catch but she knew they were talking about her.

"Hi there sweetheart." The sweet old lady said to Liv taking her new seat in 23C. "What's your name?"

"Who, me? I'm Liv."

"What a pretty name Liv. My name is Judy."

The plane rocked side to side and the seatbelt sign chimed on again. The Drunk Slob woke with the grace of a dead herring.

"Don't forget to buckle up." Liv reminded the old lady.

"Oh yes of course." Grandma buckled up and shared a romantic look with the Drunk who returned her favor. "Safety first."

Liv winced, pain shooting through her like lightning, stronger than anything before. She folded her hands into her thighs and lifted them back up to reveal blood slick crimson. To her horror she had bled through her pants. Her blood slick fingers trembled. Just then the plane took a MASSIVE NOSE DIVE. It was complete bedlam, mixed drinks and laptops flew up and into the air. Everyone was screaming bloody murder. THE HORROR. The Bride, sans seatbelt, was ejected up and out of her seat like a loaded slingshot and cracked the top of her tiara'd head on an overhead bin. She came crashing back down in a pool of her own blood and tequila nips. Her head was an absolute GuShEr. Blood poured down her face and down her white veil and all over her white pants staining them crimson. Her Delta sisters were no help, they just kept screaming and hollering. The Bride stared at the mess of blood on her hands and her gown and screamed bloody fucking murder!

II

WESTCOAST CUSTOMS

The Bride bawled like a hungover baby. The Mexican sun hit her hard as she stumbled down the airstairs and onto the tarmac. She was escorted down by 4 of her salty sorority sisters: Heather, Meadow, Emily A and Emily B. They were four girls in sunglasses too big for their faces.

"We've got you girly." Meadow reassured her sorority sister. "Hold on to us."

"Fuck this, I'm suing!" The Bride sobbed. "This is the worst day, the worst day!" Gauze wrapped the Bride's head making her look like a Halloween mummy. She donned a fresh Delta Epsilon Delta sweatshirt so that was an upgrade at least.

"Don't worry, we'll get you through customs." Heather nodded, her eyes on the customs building like it was the promised land.

"We'll get you your bags." Emily A cut in.

"Fuck my bags!" The Bride snapped.

"And we'll take you to a real doctor, not some wannabe on the plane." Meadow reassured her.

"A real doctor? In Mexico?" The Bride's eyes bugged out of her eye sockets framed with fake lashes. "No thank you! I don't need some coked-out Mexican douchebag doctor looking up my asshole! Fuck that, fuck customs and fuck my bags."

"No bags?" Emily A blinked. "But our outfits?"

Nearby, a prop plane taxied way too close for comfort. It's blades spun like they craved fresh blood. Liv saw it coming and stepped back avoiding the oncoming danger. Her foot wedged in a pothole, stuck.

"You're right," The Bride muttered, changing her tone. "I can't think."

"Don't think!" Meadow shouted over the commotion of the airport. "We've got you covered girl!"

Liv yanked her foot free from the pothole, looked up and came face to face with the Bride.

"Don't just stand there Liv! Let's go!" The Bride spat.

Inside the terminal, the customs line crawled. The girls stumbled like survivors of a pink fashion week gone bad. Two more Delta Sisters were there to meet them, beguiling and bubbly Becky and total badass Brazil. Beguiling meaning charming in a deceptive way, and bubbly meaning like bubbles. Brazil had her iPhone out already recording the rendezvous.

"Oh my god! There she is!" Brazil squeaked. "Our bride-to-be is in Tulum bitches!" And Heather squealed like a stuck piggie and gave Becky a big fat hug. High pitched hysteria. Meadow joined in and then the Bride who could barely hold herself upright. The din was nauseating. Brazil pinched and zoomed in with her camera to the Bride. "The most MVP Bride I know - wait, oh my God, what happened to your head?" Becky had her phone out now, selfie mode with the group.

"Get that shit out of my face!" The Bride snapped, emotions more topsy turvy than a taco stuck in a turnstile. "I look fucking terrible!" Smack! Her hand connected with Brazil's phone, and Brazil's phone connected with the floor. It skidded and got kicked by a tourist with a rolling duffel. Bonafide terrified Becky clutched her own phone to her chest like it was a newborn babe.

"What the fuck?!" Brazil dropped to her knees and crawled between tourists who kicked her phone back and forth without a care in the world. Brazil's long painted nails scraped across the dirty linoleum and peeled the phone up from some sticky something or other right before the Drunk Slob stomped it to death. "You know this phone is my life!" She held it up. Customs police looked over at the commotion.

"Cool it Brazil." The Bride hissed. "Cut the wannabe influencer crap!"

"One hundred and twenty thousand followers isn't wannabe, bitch."

"And did those followers come before or after the OnlyFans?"

"Wow..."

Liv gave Meadow a look like get me out of here. The customs police were walking toward them. Meadow elbowed Brazil hard in the arm. "Keep it tranquilo Brazil. We're being watched. Let's just get our girl through customs."

Brazil forced a smile as the customs police hovered over them. "You're right. I'm being harsh." She faked. "You've been through a lot, I can tell."

"I forgive you." The Bride nodded like royalty and the cops moved on and the customs line dragged on.

Becky leaned over to Heather asking her "But really... what happened?" And Heather shrugged.

"Turbulence."

"Not turbulence," the Bride barked. "Sabotage. That stewardess. That captain. The whole fucking airline is against me! They wanted to ruin my vacation, my bachelorette party. Everyone's getting sued. My man is a prosecutor."

Becky leaned over to Brazil this time. "I thought her fiancé was in finance?" She whispered.

"He is." Brazil answered.

Passports got stamped like factory meat. Thunk. Thunk. Thunk. Liv stepped up next. Bright eyed Becky turned to her, all teeth. "It's Trish isn't it?" She squeaked.

"Who me?" Liv dug through her black leather clutch stitched with metal studs. "No, it's Liv. I'm Liv."

A customs agent looked her up and down, turning a fake smile to a frown. Liv was fit and curvy but hid it under baggy clothes. "Welcome to Mexico, how long will you be visiting?"

"Just a couple of days." She handed him her passport.

Becky's voice jumped an octave. "Oh my God, Liv! The maid of honor. The childhood friend? I'm Becky, Delta sister. So good to finally meet you." Becky went in for a hug. "First time in Tulum?"

Liv smiled tight. "Yeah, first time."

"Stop!" Brazil was just behind them. "You're telling me you have never been to Tulum? It is mind altering. It is life changing. Love your outfit by the way."

"Thanks."

"Great style. What is this jacket?"

"Not sure, I got it thrifting."

Brazil's eyes lit up. "Oh my god! Vintage! So, so cute!"

"Thrifting, cool. Good for the environment."

"Reduce, reuse, recycle," said Liv.

"All black in Mexico, girl, you are gonna burn up." Meadow said to Liv without a shred of sarcasm. The customs agent stamped passports in a rhythm. Metal on paper. Paper on desk. One after the other like a machine worker punching rivets into a steel beam.

III

ZONA ROJA, ZONA BLANCA

The moving walkway dragged them through the sterile guts of the airport. Flickering fluorescents in the shadows. Hard sunlight cut through tall windows in blinding beams. Glossy tiles here and there. The echo of sandals slapping linoleum. The PA system in the airport was two voices in Spanish, one male and one female, arguing about the red zone and the white zone? The girls didn't bother to listen.

Becky leaned in close to Liv, pulling her cheap sunglasses down to the rim of her schnoz. "So, what's up first on the schedule?"

Liv blinked. "Today? Oh, just get ready I think."

"Fun!" Becky clapped like a trained seal.

The Bride snapped her neck like a snake, her fake tan glowing like a threat. "Just?"

"Sorry." Liv mumbled to the Bride. "There's a lot on my mind."

The Bride pointed to the gauze wrapped around her pulsating head. "You see this Liv? You don't think there is a lot on my mind. My head is fucking killing me!"

"I'm sorry for what happened to you. You didn't deserve it."

The Bride narrowed her eyes. "Why would I deserve it?"

"I said you didn't." Liv winced, gut-wrenching pain and a flash of red in her mind's eye.

"Are you ok?" Becky asked, rubbing Liv's shoulder.

"Yeah, fine. Just cramps."

"So, tell us!" Emily A asked the Bride as they continued down the narrow moving walkway. "What's his name, this lawyer of yours? Or are you going to keep us guessing?" Emily B bumped Emily A's arm and gestured a shush.

The Bride snapped to the Emilys. "Are you kidding me? Who talked!?"

"Andre!" The Emilys answered in sync like ugly ventriloquist dummies.

"Are you seeing someone else?" Liv asked the Bride in disbelief.

"Don't be so naive, Liv. Everyone I know is seeing someone else. That is so Andre! That boy can't keep a secret."

Liv blinked. "Who's Andre?"

"Who's Andre?!" The Emilys said in sync.

"That's totally something Andre would say!" Emily A howled.

"Listen, keep it to yourself girls." The Bride told them dead calm. "Don't yell it out. All of Mexico doesn't need to know!"

Liv watched the sun pass behind a single cloud. Distracted, she stumbled off the moving walkway.

Baggage control was a maze of conveyor belts, rubber highways, suitcases sliding like corpses on an autopsy tray. Workers inspected a broken bag, contents spilled out on the ground like entrails from roadkill. And at baggage claim the girls clustered around the carousel, fidgeting, scrolling, fixing up their makeup. "What's taking so long!" Hurry-up-Heather tapped her pudgy toes.

"Right? I mean how hard can it be to unload a bag?" The Bride crossed her arms. Her voice was acid. "Just do your job already!"

"Oh, I see mine." Liv squinted her eyes past the crowd, finding her black suitcase on its way to the chute.

"Finally." The Bride sighed and the suitcase shot down the chute like a torpedo, slammed into a metal rail like a car crash, BANG! Two wheels shattered, plastic shrapnel flying past Meadow's eyeball by a quarter inch.

"Jesus Christ!" Meadow ditched and ducked, blonde hair whipping in the Mexican sun.

Brazil had her phone out again, never missing an opportunity for fresh content. "Wow, hey followers. For those of you just joining, we are here in Tulum..."

"Just my luck." Liv sighed.

"Cursed." The Bride didn't blink.

Two unknown burly hands covered Liv's eyes, a man stood behind her. "Guess who?" He said melodically.

Liv spun, reflex, open palm SLAPPED a soft and stubbled cheek.

"Ow!" Said Bart, chubby and cute. He pinched his nose, waiting for a nosebleed that never came.

"Oh my God Bart!" Liv gasped. "Don't sneak up on me like that!"

"We'll I've never been one for an entrance." He said muffled.

"Who is that?" Meadow asked the Bride.

The Bride lit up. "Oh my God Bart! Bart! Girls this is Bart, Bart, girls. Bart is my gay best friend!"

Heather blinked. "I thought Andre was our GBF..."

"Yes," said the Bride and she went on like she was explaining a wine pairing. "Andre's our GBF from college, and Bart is my GBF from childhood. Andre is the wild type and Bart is so, so chill. This trip is big enough for the two of them!"

Bart rolled his eyes.

"I'm so sorry about the slap." Liv said to him.

"It's nothing major." He released his grip on his nose and waved it off.

"Oh my God Bart, how long has it been?" The Bride grinned like a sly she-devil.

Bart scanned the group like he was calculating odds of survival amongst these jackals, winked at Liv and nodded. "Oh, you know, like forever! Nice to meet you all girls. What the hell happened to your head?"

"Don't ask." The Bride was pissed.

"Have you met Andre yet?" Emily A stepped up.

"Who's Andre?" Bart asked.

Emily A and Emily B looked into each other's dull eyes caked with mascara and giggled like schoolgirls "Who's Andre! That is totally something Andre would say!"

"He's our you." Heather grinned.

"Oh I get it. We gays are a dime a dozen."

"Not to say there isn't room enough for two GBFs on one bachelorette. It's going to be perfect."

"I guess we'll find out."

"Alright followers, thanks for tuning in!" Brazil ended her stream, phone in pocket.

Bart looked back at Liv and mouthed 'What the fuck?'

IV
BIENVENIDAS A MÉXICO

The Bride and Meadow and the rest of the crew stood in the middle of the airport street like they owned the place. The sun baked the concrete. The sun baked the caked-on makeup on the girlies. The air was as hot and as thick as a sopa de tortilla. The smell of diesel exhaust and melting tar was all around, and the din of traffic and construction was constant. You get the picture. Meadow had her phone out, dialed a number and held it up to her pierced ear. "Hola, hi yes. Um... Hablas ingles? Great. Ok, um we are at pickup location B, terminal A."

"No, we're at pickup location A, terminal B." Heather butted in.

"What's taking so long!" The Bride hovered over her like a hungry vulture.

"No, we're not at- no nada, nothing. Hello? Not there! Here!" Meadow kept on.

"What are they saying?" The Bride asked, annoyed with Spanish as a concept.

Just then a suspicious looking priest came around the corner suspiciously. He was in black robes, too hot for the weather. Sweat drenched and sweat dripped down his sweaty brow. His eyes were down and he clutched a bible tight to his chest like someone might snatch it away from him. He walked past Liv and Bart and they caught his toxic body odor. He had tried to cover up his stench with cheap caustic cologne. He smelled like old tamales dipped in rubbing alcohol. Just then a bird shit right on Liv's shoe. Splat. Could things get any worse?

"Oh fuck." Bart held a hand to his mouth.

"Figures." Liv didn't flinch, looking down at the white mess on her black leather shoe.

"Are you fucking kidding me? Flying rat!" The Bride cawed.

"You know what," Meadow laughed, holding her phone up. "I think it's an improvement."

"Cursed." The Bride sighed.

The priest kept on keeping on, looking both ways like a feral cat searching for a meal. A pickup truck rolled past, a white limo trailed behind it. The priest didn't take his eyes off of the prize and bumped right into the Bride.

"Um, excuse me!" The Bride barked at the smelly priest.

"Disculpe." He muttered with his head down.

"Disculpe bitch!"

"Puta." He spat.

"Puta madre!" She yelled back at him.

Out from the airport out walked Boss Antonio of the Quintana Roo Cartel. He wore a suave buttoned silk shirt, a Rolex watch, and a pair of Persol sunglasses. The white limo pulled up to the curb to pick him up. The priest had found his target, opened his bible. No scripture inside, just a hollowed-out hole and a silenced pistol. He was no priest, he was a hitman of La Familia Yucatán cartel, and his target had arrived.

The smelly priest hitman pulled out his silenced pistol and took aim at his sworn enemy: Boss Antonio of the Quintana Roo Cartel. The hitman clicked the trigger, but just a click. The gun JAMMED! The hitman blinked, then all hell broke loose. From the truck three cartel men sprung out, machine guns in tow with no hesitation, no mercy. A hail of automatic gunfire and the hitman's body was thrown to the gunfire meat grinder. With each bullet blood and flesh tore off of his body and spray painted the sidewalk red. His jaw was ripped off his body, and teeth sprayed bull's-eye right into a trash can.

"GET DOWN!" Liv shouted grabbing the Bride and pulling her hard to the pavement. All of the girls and Bart dropped down. All except Becky. Becky stood and stared, eyes locked to Miguel, the driver of the tan truck. He was tall and dark and handsome and drenched in violence and mystery. In that bloody massacre of a moment time stopped for the two lovebirds. Bullets laced the air. Becky didn't blink, didn't duck. One look, one moment and the two of them knew. They were meant for each other.

"Becky fucking duck!" The Bride screamed, yanking Becky's ankle. She fell to the ground.

Boss Antonio jumped into the limo. The cartel men emptied their machine guns and piled into the pickup truck, reloading. Miguel peeled out leaving a wake of brake dust and gunpowder. When that cleared all that was left was a 'priest' in pieces. Liv's hair had a bit a blood, a bit of dirt and a bit of bird shit. Bienvenido a México, Liv.

V

ALL-INCLUSIVE

To the naked eye, Liv's hotel room was too clean. But if you had a black light, the sheets would tell you a different story. Cum stains don't wash out so easy. Everything in that room was pastel and ugly. The walls were covered in wallpaper with palm trees and pyramids. The flooring was carpeted hot pink that felt like sandpaper. Everything screamed all-inclusive with hidden fees. The Bride would end up loving this place, Liv was sure of it. But then again, that must have been why she booked it. Liv hadn't even looked at pictures on the resort's website when she booked her room with Bart. She had just followed the Bride's instructions in the email.

Liv unpacked but wished she hadn't. It would be easier to book a ticket home now than face the inevitable hell and misfortune set before her. Bart was already in a bathrobe, plush white and regal. "I have no words." He said to her. "But we're here."

"Is this how this trip is going to go?"

"Fuck it, we do it live."

Liv winced. Deep pain in her pelvis like a punishment from hell.

"Liv, are you alright?" Bart asked.

"Yeah, fine. Just my time of the month. Talk about bad timing."

"Let's just relax, babe. I'll hop in the shower first then you. Traveling did me dirty!"

Liv checked her groin, dry to the touch. "Same."

Knock! Knock! Someone was at the door. The two froze in time, eyes met and panic set. "Don't open it." She whispered, but Bart rolled his eyes and opened the door and there he was. Tall. Dark. Handsomer than Miguel. Andre was sculpted like a Greek statue. His figure was ripped right out of a Calvin Klein ad. He leaned back on his Louis Vuitton suitcase, and they could smell his sweet cologne. Everything else on him was Armani except his shades. His Persols hid light eyes on a face like Michael B. Jordan's.

"Hi there." Andre said, smooth like jazz and liqueur.

"Hi there yourself." Bart melted but kept it sarcastic as usual.

"I'm Andre, and you are?" Andre tilted his glasses down showing off light eyes. Must have been contacts.

"Oh, me? Bart. I'm Bart. Friends with Liv. Friends of the Bride."

"Charmed." The two shook hands. Passionate, strong, yet supple. "And you must be Liv. Bart and Liv. I've heard a lot about you two."

"And we've heard a lot about you," said Liv.

"So, I've heard." Andre took off his shades, too cool for school. He stepped inside, scanned the room like he was going to make an offer to buy it. "Not bad, not bad at all. This will do." Then he plopped his bags on the bed that had been Liv's.

"Are you rooming with us?" Liv asked, annoyed but trying to hide that she was so fucking annoyed that she might be misconstrued as a bitch. She was no bitch.

"Apparently this shithole of a resort overbooked," Andre lied. "Looks like I'll be staying with you two. Hope you don't mind."

"No, not at all!" Bart said, smitten.

"Good. Listen, I could really use a shower."

"I was just about to hop in for a rinse," said Bart. "I won't be long."

"Should I jump in with you?" Andre didn't miss a beat. "Save water, save the planet. Reduce, reuse, recycle."

Bart looked back at Liv, eyes wide, jaw unhinged. "Handsome and climate conscious!" Bart squealed.

Andre was all fours rummaging through the mini bar. "Kidding." He said, "You get in there. I gotta unpack and get my shit together. Big dinner tonight. Dress to impress and I mean to impress. Right Liv?"

Liv nodded. "Right."

"Right." Bart added, practically skipping to the bathroom. He mouthed 'oh my god' before slamming the door shut. Now it was just Liv and Andre in awkward silence. Andre stood up holding two spiked seltzers, cracked one open and handed the closed one to Liv.

"So are you the one that used to play dress up with our bride-to-be?" He asked. "Looks like you traded in the tutus and tiaras for a buy-one-get-one coupon at Hot Topic. No offense or nothing."

Liv cracked her drink open and took a sip. "None taken. You're not that far off anyway. Did your cologne bottle break in transit, or do you usually smother yourself in it like a cheap prostitute?"

Andre laughed. "You're too cute."

"How much are these anyway?" Liv held up the can.

"It's all-inclusive girly" Andre waved it off. "Don't worry about it." Liv glanced at the minibar menu. Ten dollars for water, fifteen for beer. Bart was singing in the shower now, water running full blast. "Liv." Andre asked her.

"Yes?"

He sat on the bed he had claimed with his Louis Vuitton luggage. "Tell me about Brad, he is so my type." He crossed his well-muscled legs.

"You mean Bart." She corrected. "He's your type?"

"Yes Bart! Tell me everything!"

"Well." She said, sipping her cold, sugary, boozy beverage. "Where do I begin..."

VI

ITINERARY REPORT

The Bride's hotel room was a hot mess. Nine girls, two bottles of tequila and a curling iron set to scorch. Cheap drinks, cheap fashion and cheap lip gloss streaked across cracked lips injected with cheap filler. The girlies traded outfits that smelled like an airport lavatory. Two of them argued about who had the better playlist and played some throwback bullshit on a Bluetooth speaker.

The Bride peeled back the sticky bandage on her forehead, revealing a gash. It was pink, raw and nasty. "Do you think this needs stitches?" She asked hepatitis Heather.

"I mean, your bangs hide it pretty well." Heather squinted through a mascara haze. Emily A hit a wax pen running on empty and passed it to Emily B.

"Shit, what even was that?" Emily B took the final drag and exhaled. "Like a cartel war? This town is a shit hole!"

"We should have gone to Nashville." Emily A sing-songed.

"Girls! Enough!" The bride adjusted her smothered boobs in an overtight bra. "This is the last I'll hear of it, ok? It didn't happen. No more negativity on this trip. This is my party. This is my weekend! We need to chill the fuck out!"

"Fine, sorry." Emily A muttered. "Forget it." And poured a shot of tequila for herself that Brazil grabbed.

"Tilt that head back, this will disinfect anything." Brazil instructed the Bride, half joking, half serious. She looked ready for surgery.

"Hell no, give it here." The Bride took the shot and downed it in one go, clean, no flinch and the girls all cheered. "I'm not wasting a good buzz on this cut. It's fine. Now pour another round for my girlies Brazil. We're here to celebrate!"

"DELTAS! DELTAS!" The girls cheered, shots were poured in dick shaped glasses, they clinked, downed them, faces flush.

"Yes! Now this is the energy I needed!" The Bride screamed. "You girls are absolutely killing it."

"Liv has some catching up to do." Meadow stated the obvious.

"What did you say?" The Bride gave Meadow the dirty side-eye.

"I said Liv has some catching up to do." Meadow stood her ground. "Like where even is your maid of honor?"

"Getting ready I guess." The Bride checked herself out in a mirror.

"But not ready enough to get ready with us?" Meadow stated the obvious.

"Bleak." Halitosis-Heather backed up Meadow, always her little minion. But the years of excess and binge drinking had done her dirty. She was not so little anymore.

"And how did she pull the maid of honor title anyway?" Meadow asked, words like poison. "Is she closer to you than us girls? And that dreadful style of hers, what even is that? Emo?"

"Double bleak."

"She's going through some things, ok?" The Bride defended her friend. "Her boyfriend just broke up with her and stuff. But you guys! She's like my oldest friend. She's no Delta... but she's one of us."

"Yet she's not here." Meadow rubbed it in.

Becky mutilated her hair with a scorching hot curling iron. "Cut her some slack, Meadow! She seems so sweet!"

"Maybe she just needs to get laid." Emily A pointed out the obvious.

"Where is she so we can cheer her up!" Becky yelped.

"She's with the boys." The Bride answered. "They're all bunking together on account of Andre not booking a room like he was supposed to. That boy had the audacity to think he'd be sharing a room with me! Like no queen, I need my R and R."

"Are you serious?" Meadow asked.

"He's such a moocher." The Bride giggled.

"He's such a moocher!"

"That's so Andre," Emily A chimed in.

"So-" Heather stepped in, "Liv's sleeping single in a single bed with two queens in a queen bed. I love it."

The Deltas laughed, shrill and echoing. A work friend Alexa blinked. "Wait hold up. Are you saying there are men on this trip? How posh!"

"Yes, my two gay best friends." The Bride answered. "One from college, the other from childhood. Trust me, you'll love them."

"I didn't know someone could have two gay best friends!"

"You know me, I'm greedy. I collect them like baseball cards." The Bride chuckled. "And Liv is living la vida loca with them on this trip!" Sparse laughs. Forced. The doors opened and Liv walked in. Everyone stopped and turned.

"Speak of the devil." Meadow was deadpan and took another sip of her drink. Her eyes piercing. Heather stuck out her tongue and made devil horns with her fingers. "Stop it!" Meadow laughed, hitting her little.

"Hi everyone." Liv looked around the room, feeling like she was on the wrong side of the fence at a zoo.

"Play nice girlies," said the Bride. "Oh my little Devil you! My maid of honor herself! How are you? Tell me, where are the boys?"

"They're still in the room."

"Oh my god." Heather leaned forward. "Don't tell me they're hooking up?"

"I... I don't think so."

"Say it ain't so!" The Bride gasped. "No way. They are not each other's types. No way!"

"Well, that's not what Andre said. He said he likes Bart."

"Liv!" Brazil jumped up. "You are kidding!"

"Nope, dead serious."

"Liv's got the gossip!" Brazil shrieked.

"I told you they would." Heather said to the Bride.

"They are not!" The Bride insisted. "Well maybe they might do stuff, maybe. But they are not hooking up!"

"What's the difference?"

"No way!"

"Oh my God, Liv!" The Bride shouted in disbelief.

"Yes?"

"Gross. Let's change the subject. The itinerary. Liv, please tell the girls what we have scheduled for this week."

"Oh yeah sure. Yeah, ok hold on." She held in her stomach and grunted.

"You feeling ok?" The Bride asked.

"Yeah, just crampy."

"Bad timing!" The Bride winked at Meadow, their little secret. Liv went for her phone, fumbling. Meadow beat her to it with itinerary print outs, no need for that digital nonsense. Old school baby, on floral card stock no less. Wedding font. She passed them out like bulletins to the church of Satan.

"Girls, I've got printouts." Meadow announced like it was her show. "And for those of you who lose them, I'll forward you the link to our website. So, we have as follows-" They went down the list.

Wednesday: *Welcome Wednesday. Wear your best. Dress to impress. Hibachi Welcome Dinner.*

"Hibachi in Mexico?" Alexa interrupted.

"Oh, they do it so good here." Heather answered.

"No more interruptions." Meadow was so annoyed.

Thursday: *Neon Thirst Trap Thursday. Brunch. Pool. Sun. Dinner. Clubbing.*

Friday: *Sun Fried Friday. Naughty and Nautical. Yacht. Beach Dinner. Black out in all black at the club.*

Saturday: *Sexy Safari Saturday. Pole Dancing Class. Poolside lunch. Concert. Bonfire and S'mores.*

Sunday: *Spa Recovery. Manis. Pedis. Saunas. Cold plunges. Maybe a happy ending.*

"Unless you are flying out early - in which case too bad because secret night out," said Meadow. "And Liv, you'll love blackout in all black! That's so your style!"

"Wow, wow, wow!" The Bride jumped in. "This is perfection!" She swigged her drink. "The only thing missing is something stronger than this shit."

"What do you have in mind?"

"My plug Sanguine Rose." The Bride said, salivating. "Arrives tomorrow morning with the party favors. God, I love her!" Becky's hot curling iron slid off the table, no one noticed. The carpet singed and smoked.

"This Rose girl sounds amazing." Said Brazil. "Who is she?"

"Sanguine Rose. I met her at EDC three years ago and we hit it off at the after's. We talked until the sunrise, then we just kept dancing until the sunset. We're the same Zodiac sign. You want something, she's got it."

Heather leaned in to inspect the Bride's hair, stepped back and screamed: "FUCK ME!" The hot curling iron connected with her heel and cooked it medium rare. She grabbed the iron bare handed and chucked it out an open window and into the night.

"My curler!" Becky gasped.

Outside and three stories down the hot curler landed on a parked jet ski burning through its fuel line. Drip, drip, drip, the gasoline bled all over the jet ski's guts and out into the black sand.

VII

GUAC & ROLL

The Bride and her tribe of Deltas lined up at a hostess stand of "Guac & Roll", the best Japanese-Mexican fusion hibachi restaurant this side of the Gulf. There was a koi pond and a tacky stone statue of a buddha holding up a margarita. The girls were all glitter and self-tanner, all dolled up in their Wednesday Best. Liv wore her signature black. They were all hungry and, worst of all, sobering up.

Liv leaned in over the hostess table. "Hi yes, excuse me." She got the host's attention. "Yes. Reservation for our bachelorette party. Table for fourteen."

"Thirteen now." Heather hobbled over. "Ashleigh couldn't make it."

"Thirteen." Liv corrected.

"Couldn't make it is a nice way of saying fucking flaked." The Bride said indignantly, which is a fancy word for being annoyed.

"Oh no!" Becky jumped in. "Ash couldn't make it?"

"But it's twelve tonight. Sanguine Rose comes tomorrow. Count much?"

"Tomorrow couldn't come sooner." Emily A sighed.

"You're telling me."

Emily B blinked. "Isn't thirteen like an unlucky number or something?"

"Yeah." Alexa chimed in with the confidence of an outdated Wikipedia page. "Of course it is! That's why some buildings don't have a thirteenth floor."

"Can you say that part again for my followers?" Brazil asked with her phone out livestreaming.

The Bride snapped like a guillotine. "What did I fucking say, Brazil? No negativity. Put that fucking phone away. I'll tell you when I want a photo." She fluffed her greasy hair and scratched the swollen gash on her forehead.

"It was live." Brazil ended the stream.

"Twelve, it will be twelve now." Liv told the hostess and the hostess led the pack of hungry she-wolves through the kitschy restaurant.

"Hibachi in Mexico?" Bart whispered to Liv.

"Apparently it's her favorite."

The table was decorated like a cheap nightmare. Balloons, penis straws, photos of the husband-to-be on large printouts. And at the head of the table, a blow-up sex doll, dildo and all, with the husband-to-be's face printed out and taped to its plastic head.

"Oh my God, you girls!" The Bride gasped. "This is too perfect!"

Meadow beamed. "The restaurant let us set it up earlier!"

"This is too perfect!" The Bride beamed back. "Absolutely fabulous! Thank you, girlies! Now sit, sit! Everyone sit!"

The group collapsed into their chairs. Liv got stuck between Bart and Alexa. Tight squeeze and fake smiles. Alexa leaned in. "It's Liv, right? I'm Alexa, the work friend."

"Hi Alexa, nice to meet you. Have you met Bart?"

The two strangers shook hands across Liv's chest, nearly knocking over her water glass.

"What are you gonna get?" The Emilys asked each other simultaneously. A busboy filled water cups.

"This better not be tap!"

"Um just like a California roll or something."

The Bride wasn't having it. "No come on Emily! It's hibachi night! You must get the steak and shrimp combo. It's the absolute best!"

Tanya, the Brides' big and eldest Delta there, stiffened up. "No shrimp for me, I'm allergic."

"Have you been here before?" Alexa asked the Bride but was ignored.

"You have to try the shrimp, Tanya!" The Bride went on. "It's got to be so fresh here in Mexico!"

Tanya's voice dropped to a dead serious tone. "I'm serious. I'm like deathly allergic to shellfish. Don't you remember? As my little you should remember. We're supposed to be sisters." And the table went silent. There were cheers from a nearby table where a chef did the onion volcano. Tanya cracked a smile. "Just kidding girly! It's fine you forgot."

"Oh, thank God." The Bride sighed and everyone laughed all bubbly like.

"I guess I just don't get your guy's sense of humor." Alexa commented confused.

"But for real like I'm deathly allergic." Tanya said under her breath. "I shouldn't even be here."

The conversation droned on and on and Liv checked out for a bit while the chef did his magic. Fire licked the ceiling, rice was chopped up into egg, shrimp flew through the air. Friends laughed and bantered. And Liv just sat there disconnected and dejected staring into the wall.

"Liv did you hear me?" The Bride asked her, breaking her soft trance.

"What?"

"I was just telling everyone about when we were kids. The pact we made. You know what, get over here! Tell everyone!" And Liv got up to join the Bride and her storytelling. She moved into the empty seat beside the Bride that had been Meadow's. Meadow was MIA. "And Bart, you were there too. Why don't you guys share the story?

Liv stiffened, uneasy. "Alright sure. I guess we were about seven years old right?"

"We can't hear you!" Someone shouted from the other side of the table.

The Bride elbowed Liv. "Stand up!"

Liv stood. "Well, we were seven."

"Louder!"

"Who is that anyway?" Tanya asked.

"How rude of me." The Bride cut in. "Let me get some introductions out of the way." She stood and her chair fell back hitting an elderly couple minding their own business. She pushed Liv back down into her seat. "Well for those of you who don't know me... Oh wait you all know me! No intro needed."

THE BRIDE: *The reason we're all here*

Deltas cheer. "Most of you are my Delta sisters." The Bride went on." The rest, honorary Deltas today. To my right, Liv. My right hand girly. Stand up Liv!"

LIV: *Maid of Honor (for now)*

"Hi everyone. Like I was saying, we were like seven." Liv continued. A toilet flushed and Meadow was back.

"And for those of you who don't know me!" Meadow butted in, with toilet paper dragging from her high heel. "I am Meadow!"

MEADOW: *Delta, the Bitch*

Meadow glared at Liv. "Keeping my seat warm I see?"

"Meadow you are the best!" The Bride laughed. "One of a kind. But simmer down bitch, I'll do the intros."

"Of course girly." Meadow loomed over Liv like a ghoul in high heels.

"Heather you're up. Oh my God, Meadow do you remember when Heather here did that keg stand at the fall mixer sophomore year? Forty-five seconds! Took five sigma tau deltas to hold you up!"

"Like I remember those STD's?" Heather laughed. "No way.

(hobbling) **HEATHER:** *Delta, Meadow's little*

The Bride went around the table rapid fire intros. "Emilys! My ride or dies!"

EMILY A and EMILY B: *Delta's Bimbos*

"Bart, the original!"

BART: *Childhood GBF*

"Alexa, I don't know if I'd even show up on Monday at the office if it wasn't for you."

ALEXA: *Work Friend... dull*

"Andre, you came into my life late and when I needed you the most. Boy if you weren't gay I'd probably have married you myself!"

"In your dreams." Andre sucked down a cocktail.

ANDRE: *College GBF*

"Becky, Becky. The absolute life of the party and my little. I love you."

BECKY: *Delta, Bride's little*

"Tanya, the one who showed me the ropes. Remember that summer at the lake? Actually, better if we forget it!"

"What are you talking about?" Tanya truly did forget.

TANYA: *Delta, Bride's big*

"Thank you, thank you all so much for being here! Now Liv, tell them about our pact!" The Bride lifted Liv back up with drunk strength.

"She forgot me?" Brazil stood up and left quietly.

BRAZIL: *Delta, Cursed and forgotten*

Flashback and we find ourselves out in a grassy field, summer light bleeding through thick maple trees. The Bride was just a little girl then with her friends. She wore a makeshift veil fashioned from a silk scarf. Young Bart stood in an oversized suit jacket two sizes too big, sleeves swallowing his limbs. Liv, holding a paper towel roll like an unraveled holy scroll, stood between them officiating like she knew what she was doing.

"We'd play all sorts of games." Liv told the group in the present day. "Dress up, play weddings. Bart played the part of the husband."

"Marrying a woman, as if!" Bart joked.

Back in the past Liv cleared her throat. "D-dearly beloved, we are gathered today-"

"You missed a part." The young Bride cut in, hands on her hips. "Gathered HERE today."

"Sorry." Young Liv continued. "We are gathered here today to-" But before she could finish Bart's mom yelled out from the back door of the house.

"Kids! Lunch is ready!"

"Dunkaroos! Yes!" Bart lit up and tore off up to the house, suit jacket flapping in the wind.

"Bart! But we haven't been married yet!" The young Bride called after him, stomping her princess plastic heels into the grass.

"I don't like you like that!" He called back, his sly voice trailing off.

"Let's go eat." Young Liv suggested, but the young Bride grabbed Liv's hands and held them tight.

"Oh Liv, I'm just dying to get married. I can't wait for my prince charming to sweep me off my feet. Don't you want that Liv, don't you want that for me?"

"I don't know what I want. I'm just a kid." Young Liv shrugged.

"Promise me Liv." The young Bride squeezed her hands tight to her chest. "Promise me that when I get married you'll be my maid of honor. And I'll be yours. Ok?"

"Ok." Liv nodded, stomach rumbling.

So, there it was, the pact had been made. And back in the present day at Guac & Roll, that shitty sushi Mexican fusion joint, the room sat suspended in silence with the smell of old fish and burnt onion.

"And what did you say Liv?" Becky asked, holding on to every word.

"I said yes."

"She said yes!" The Bride grinned so wide you'd think her nasty lips would crack. She raised her glass high above the table. "And the rest is history girls. Now please everyone raise your glasses." And around the table drinks lifted and swayed. "To Liv! And to me!" The voices rang out together. The Bride stared at Liv from her drink, eyes haunting.

"To us." Liv took a long-needed drink.

VIII

A SHIT SHOW

Liv pushed open the door to the ladies' room. Warm lights overhead and the smell of melted makeup and cleaning products covered up someone's sick. Brazil was at the mirror freshening up her eyeliner. "Hi there." Liv greeted her when their eyes met.

"Hi there yourself." Brazil smiled as sweet as a knife tip and slammed shut her makeup kit. Liv moved down the row of stalls, finding all of them locked.

"Occupied!" A shrill voice shrieked from behind a locked stall.

"Sorry." Liv moved on to the next, a handicap stall that was wide open and inviting. Roomy with a sink and a vanity mirror, luxurious even. Liv went inside but before she could close the door Brazil pushed her way in. "What are you doing?" Liv blinked.

"Oh, grow up!" Brazil shrugged like it was obvious and made her way to the sink and vanity mirror, taking out her makeup kit. "Friends who pee together stay together. Don't let me stop your business."

"Alright." Liv sighed and locked the door. The cheap lock slid off and broke. Neither of them noticed. Liv dropped her pants and sat on the toilet. Urine mixed with blood came out. Streaks of red in the bowl.

Brazil droned on. "So, like what's her deal tonight? I mean yeah, she can be cold but... is it just me or she like extra cold. Icy. Especially to me. I mean you're her family right? What do you think?"

"No relation." Liv and the Bride looked nothing alike. "Just friends. Childhood friends."

"Exactly!" Brazil continued like she had won an argument. "That's what I'm saying! No family here at all? That's suspicious as fuck and you know it. I know it. Maybe you can tell me. I heard she had a major falling out with her family and hasn't talked to them in years. Is it true?"

Liv wiped, flushed, and pulled up her jeans and moved to the sink. "I don't like to gossip." Brazil turned on the faucet for her. "Thanks."

Brazil unzipped her jorts, pulled them down and sat on the still warm toilet seat. Liv ran cold water down her hands, fingernails painted black and silver. In the bathroom, an elderly woman in a wheelchair peeked low under the stall door, sighed and rolled away.

"It's not gossip." Brazil's voice softened, fishing for answers. "It's just girl talk. So, tell me if I'm right."

"I'm not confirming or denying." Liv turned off the faucet and dried her hands.

"Well, I heard she's sleeping with her sister's ex-fiancé." Brazil didn't know when to stop and she couldn't help herself from going on. "I heard her family disowned her for it. I heard her husband-to-be has no clue. No clue! Total idiot. I heard she's fooled him into thinking her whole family is a bunch of abusive alcoholics, meanwhile her dad is some hot shot attorney who doesn't even drink!"

BANG! The door to the handicap stall burst open, lock falling to the ground like a bullet casing, and standing there red faced and fuming was the Bride. Her eyes were like open wounds.

"What's this shit!" She spat. "Some sort of shit talking potty party?"

"Oh hey girl!" Brazil jumped off the toilet mid stream, pulling up her pants. Wet stains crept down her jorts. "We were just-"

"Shut it Brazil." The Bride held up a violent finger. "I heard everything you said." Then she turned to Liv. "And you, Liv. My own maid of honor. Talking shit about me behind my back at my own bachelorette party? Wow. I expected more from you."

"I-" Liv couldn't come up with anything else to say.

"Enough." And the Bride leaned into Brazil so close they could smell each other's stanking breath, tequila and enzymed lime. "You want the truth Brazil?" The Bride's voice dropped low, slow and lethal. "Yea, everything you said? That's right. I get what I want. I take what's mine. And the people that get in my way? I cut out. And you. Are. Cut. Out!"

Liv stood frozen. Brazil had tears welling up in her eyes. A relationship flushed down the toilet.

IX
THE QUINTANA ROO PLAN

The air was thick with cigar smoke somewhere at a super secret compound. A light hung high above a wood table in an industrial room. Dark shadows. Ten cartel men of the Quintana Roo sat around that table. All of them were hard men. Each of them had killed before they celebrated their own quinceañeras. All of them were high-ranking soldiers. There was Boss Antonio, and his Underboss. Then there was the killer handsome Miguel, lusting after Becky in his mind's eye. The rest were soldiers.

In the corner of the room was some tied up poor soul bloodied up, hooded, and gagged. He'd been tortured for days. A table lay beside him with bloodied pliers, wires, razors and saws.

"Those Yucatán dogs grow bold." Boss Antonio rose and spoke, voice low. His Spanish like gravel rolling off a dump truck.

"They grow desperate." The Underboss banged his meaty fist against the wooden table.

"I hear they hide in the jungles now. Scared!" A soldier added.

"We burnt them out." Miguel cracked his knuckles. "Those monkeys got nowhere left to go but back to the trees."

"Are they monkeys or dogs?" A soldier asked.

"They are dogs and monkeys!" Boss Antonio laughed. "Not men. Not anymore. To attack us in broad daylight at the airport? Dressed up like a fucking priest? Where do they get off? There's no honor in that." Boss Antonio spat on the ground. "The Yucatán are a dying breed."

"So, we hit them back hard!" Another soldier said.

"If we can find them." Miguel shrugged.

"You're a good hound dog Miguel," The Underboss lit another cigar. "Maybe you can sniff them out."

"So now I'm a dog too?" Miguel's smile curled.

Boss Antonio crossed the room and placed a heavy hand on Miguel's shoulder. Aztec ink bled up and down his hairy arms. "You're a wolf Miguel." He reassured him, his grip squeezing like an anaconda. "A wolf of the Quintana Roo Cartel. Never forget it." And Boss Antonio released his tight grip and turned and walked to the tied up prisoner. "Gentlemen.... remember we are fighting a war on two fronts. We have to stay vigilant." His hand hovered over the tray of torture tools. He grabbed a syringe filled with yellow poison and drove the needle into the prisoner's neck. The body convulsed, twitched, groaned and then went limp. Dead. Boss Antonio washed his hands in a slop sink. "And ruthless."

"But boss, couldn't we have used that CIA agent as leverage?" A soldier asked.

"No." Boss Antonio dried his hands with a rag. "I got all I needed out of him. Everything important at least." He smirked. "And guess what he told me?"

"What did he say, boss?" The Underboss asked.

Antonio's smile widened. "He told me the feds are sending a whole team down here. Multiple agencies. They will be hiding in plain sight, dressed as tourists. Elderly couples, bachelorette parties even. We need to keep a sharp eye. They could be young beautiful women, vixens trained to seduce you, drain you of your information and kill you. No remorse, no hesitation." He grabbed a bottle of tequila and poured himself a drink. "I want the beaches watched. The hotels watched. I want a man at every one of our bars, clubs, hotels and restaurants. Eyes everywhere, gentlemen!"

"It would be my honor to be your eyes, Boss Antonio." Miguel stood.

"Good. I want you at the hotels Miguel. Stay vigilant. Stay ruthless."

Miguel bowed his head. "Anything for you, Boss Antonio."

X

COUNTING SHEEPLE

In her hotel room, Liv climbed into the bed she shared with Bart, feeling defeated. In the other bed Andre was passed out, mouth agape, snoring loud enough to crack the drywall. Bart turned to face Liv in the dark. "Are you alright?" He asked her. "You've been real quiet since dinner."

Liv swallowed, then let it out. "I want to go home. I think she hates me."

Bart pulled the blanket tight around his shoulders. "If you leave me here to fend for myself with these hyenas, I swear to God..."

"These girls are fucking wretched."

"Yeah, well what did you expect from our blushing bride to be." Bart snorted.

Liv pulled her pillow tight. "Let's just leave together. You and me. We'll book flights first thing in the morning."

"You're the maid of honor," Bart reminded her. "You can't just get up and leave."

"She's going to demote me, I know it. After all the stuff with Brazil and the way Meadow is gunning for the job. I know it."

"Don't sweat it, even if she did demote you, would that really be such bad of a thing?"

"I guess not... It's just embarrassing."

"Who cares what those bitches think. Just take your mind off of it. What's on the agenda for tomorrow then?"

Liv stared out the window dreaming of a way out. "It's Neon Thirst Trap Thursday. Brunch is at 10am."

"Well, there you go!" Bart grinned in the dark. "We'll get our food on, we'll get our drink on, we'll get our mood, and-"

"And our sleep on!" Andre interrupted, his voice hoarse and wicked and half asleep. "If you two don't shut the fuck up I'm kicking you out. Andre needs his beauty sleep."

"Sorry Andre."

"No problem, babies. Just shut the fuck up and go to bed." Andre jostled and threw a pillow over his head.

"Goodnight Liv." Bart whispered turning over and getting comfy.

"Goodnight Bart." Liv sighed. The moonlight leaked in through the curtains. Liv stared out to a full moon, big, cold and ever watching. Out on the beach and under that moonlit sky the burnt and wounded jet ski leaked gasoline. Drip. Drip. Drip.

XI

KISSED BY A SANGUINE ROSE

Sanguine Rose's beat-up Jeep Wrangler ate dust down the twisties of Tulum. Tulum burned at noontime like an Easy-Bake oven lamp. Sun cracked and peeling. Sanguine Rose had the Jeep's top down. Her braided and dreaded hair whipped up like tumbleweeds in a storm. Her sunglasses were scratched, her outfit hippie-meets-techno-punk. She sang off-key with the radio that crackled when she drove in the shadow of the mountains. The lyrics were therapy for a girl who raised herself. Kissed by a rose.

A few miles down the road and she was met face to face with resort security. At a guard booth two handsome guards stood strong holding assault rifles. They smiled with silver teeth. Their green fatigues were drenched in old sweat. Sanguine Rose pulled up, flashed her passport and flashed a little skin. "Hi boys, is this valet or can I self-park? This stick shift is pretty tricky unless you know how to work it." She rubbed and tugged the transmission shift knob. The guards blushed and waved her right through. She winked at them as she passed.

At the hotel entrance, Mario the bellhop, or so said his name tag, was there to take Sanguine Rose's luggage. "Hola señora. May I assist you with your luggage?"

"Mario!" She hopped out of her Jeep, reading his nametag. "It's so amazing to see you!" She hugged him like they'd known each other for years. Mario looked over to another valet confused but they both just shrugged. "Don't worry about me Mario, all I have is this little ol' duffel and I can handle it all by myself just fine." She winked. She found a loose piece of gum in her oversized hemp-sewn sling bag and popped it in her mouth, fuzz and all.

Liv came waltzing out of the hotel's revolving doors. "Are you Sanguine Rose?" She asked.

"That's me!"

"I'm Liv, the maid of honor. I was told to meet you and get you settled in."

"Oh my God, Liv!" Sanguine Rose punched her right in the tit.

"Ow!"

"Oh sorry. My bad. I've heard so much about you, Liv!"

"Ma'am your valet ticket." Mario handed the ticket to her.

"Thank you, Mario!" She took it and blew him a kiss. She grabbed Liv by the arm and they walked and talked

"Is Mario a friend of yours?" Liv asked.

"He is now. So! Tell me everything. How was last night, what did I miss? Wait, somethings off, I can tell. You're upset. No, you upset her. How did you upset her? Wait, don't tell me. It's all going to be okay." And before Liv could answer, Sanguine Rose pulled her in for a tight hug and kissed her forehead like a drunk therapist.

"Wow. You're spot on. How'd you guess?"

"I have a way with people." The two entered the hotel. Miguel of the Quintana Roo Cartel leaned against a column dressed as a bellhop smoking a cigarette watching the two girls.

The hotel lobby was hyped up with the noise of loose children, bickering parents and drunk tweens. The air was heavy with sweat and bad decisions. The air conditioning kicked into overdrive to fight the heat and that god awful smell. Sanguine Rose and Liv passed an elderly couple booking a tour to see some ruins. Next to them was a family vacation imploding in real time.

"So how was the drive in?" Liv asked Sanguine Rose.

"Oh my god, beautiful! The scenery was gorgeous!"

"You weren't worried driving alone through Mexico?"

"I wasn't alone. Everyone I meet is an opportunity for a new friend. I've driven up and down Mexico twice, and Central and South America. Everyone I meet is so kind. So kind!" They exited the lobby and entered the vast back patio of the hotel. Dozens of fountains and man-made waterfalls, beautiful flower beds and planted palms. So many guests drenched in sunscreen and body glitter. "Look at this place!"

Sexy young men played volleyball while perverted drunk cougars watched from behind thick rimmed sunglasses. They sipped their colorful drinks. And out on the perfectly blue ocean there were jet skis, boats, and parasails. A banana float filled with sexy screaming spring breakers trailed behind a speedboat. Sexy boat drivers. Sexy sailboats. Sexy disasters waiting to happen.

The Bride and her posse in their neon thirst-trap attire lounged at the pool. Every girl looked hot by proximity. Even the ugly ones glowed among them in the Mexican sun.

"I think I know the answer..." Emily A asked Emily B looking at a lunch menu. "...But if I order fries, will you share them with me?"

"You know it! Ugh, you're my swan song." Emily B was giddy. "Excuse me, garçon?"

The Bride looked up to find her drug plug Sanguine Rose. She jumped up from her lounge chair. "Sanguine Rose! There you are!" She flip-flopped over to hug her, already wasted. "My love!"

"This is perfect!" Said Sanguine Rose. "Absolute paradise! The stars are aligned for this trip, for all of us. Hi ladies!" She greeted the group.

"Did you bring the goods?" Emily A asked her bluntly.

"Rude much?" The Bride shook her head in disapproval. "Let her settle in."

"What happened to your head?" Sanguine Rose asked the Bride.

"It's nothing." The Bride brushed her freshly botched bangs over her forehead to hide the gash. "But yeah, anyway did you bring the goods?"

"Of course." Sanguine Rose laughed and held up her sling bag.

"Listen girlie." Meadow stepped in like it was her show and Sanguine Rose was there for an audition. "I'm Meadow, our Bride's best friend. Why don't you get settled into your room, change, come back once you're... settled in! Liv can show you around, can't you Liv."

"Sure." Liv said dejected as usual.

"No bother!" And without missing a beat Sanguine Rose dropped her duffle and disrobed revealing a bright neon swimsuit. "Way ahead of you."

"Impressive!" Becky clapped.

"Hold this for safekeeping." Sanguine Rose handed Becky her car valet card, loose change, and passport like it was refuse. "Jackknife!" She yelled and was airborne and jumped into the pool with a massive splash. Brazil whipped out her phone to record.

"Oh my God, Heather just got absolutely drenched." Brazil laughed.

"Enough with the socials, Brazil!" The Bride was pissed. "Does every fucking moment need to be recorded, really?"

"Rude much?" Brazil put her phone down. "It might be your party, but you don't have to shit on my parade."

"You know what, why don't you just fuck right off Brazil?"

"Deserved." Heather backed up the Bride and was nose to nose now with Brazil. Meadow wedged in between them before it got bloody.

"You know what, Brazil." Meadow said. "Why don't you just like, go for a walk."

"Bitch." Brazil took a breath, shrugged and went for a walk.

"What did I miss?" Sanguine Rose was up from the water watching the aftermath.

"Yeah! Fuck you bitch, bye!" The Bride shouted. "Go find another party to crash. Now check this out!" The Bride cannonballed into the pool and everyone cheered.

"What was with that?" Alexa asked Tanya. "Are they like, not friends anymore or something?"

"I can't keep up." Tanya answered. Nearby and hidden under brush was an old pool forgotten by time and by the cleaning staff. A green bubbling cesspool petri dish of hotel liability. The slime pool oozed and steamed like a science experiment gone wrong.

XII

KABOOM!

Brazil liked her alone time. She needed to get away from those bitches. She strolled down the beach and scrolled away on her phone, checking out old selfies. She was hotter last summer she thought. Her battery was running dangerously low. She looked up to the beach around her. Parasails, jet skis, and sexy and unsexy people laughing and living. "Fuck it." She hyped herself up. "I'm here. I'm gonna have some fun. How much for a half hour?" She asked a bored attendant at a jet ski rental hut.

Back with the bachelorette party at the pool, Meadow had turned Sanguine Rose's jackknife jump into a full-blown contest. Heather hobbled her way in for a big ol' splash.

"Cannonball!" She shouted.

"Hobbling Heather." Bart cackled and Liv nearly drowned in her drink.

The Bride climbed out of the water, dripping wet and buzzed. "Mediocre, Heather! Becky, record this!"

"Where's Brazil?" Becky asked taking out her phone to record the Bride's big jump. "She always gets the best content."

"That bitch?" The Bride stepped back for distance. She really wanted to make this one count. "She's dead to me."

"Get a running start!" Meadow shouted, and the Bride kept on staggering backwards. Behind her like a bubbly invitation of disease and dysentery was that hidden slime pool.

And out over the water, Brazil was full throttle on her rental jet ski. It was the same jet ski that the curling iron had burned through. Sea foam and salt water splashed Brazil's hair and gasoline wept down the jet ski's sides like tears.

Back at the pool, the Bride kept walking back, and back, one step after the other closer to her slimy demise.

Back in the ocean, Brazil's jet ski's engine revved hard, coughed, sputtered, burned.

Back at the pool, the Bride took another step, teetered on oblivion, slipped and fell into the slime pool coming out of it like a diseased Nickelodeon game show contestant, screaming and drenched in green muck.

Back in the ocean, Brazil's jet ski ignited! KABOOM! A red-hot fireball quickly turned into a mushroom cloud. Jet ski shrapnel and Brazil's body parts were airborne. Her decapitated head skipped across the water like a skipping stone, right past a banana boat.

Back at the pool, the Bride was screaming bloody murder, running covered in green ooze that smelled like death. Friends grabbed towels and cloaked the screaming Bride.

"Help! Someone call 911!"

XIII

IT'S ILL TO SPEAK ILL OF THE DEAD

Hours passed, the beach grew dark, sirens. Police were taking statements like it was open mic night for trauma. "My trip is ruined!" The Bride cried. She had showered but the grime was still in her hair, and a rash was forming around her scalp.

"No it's not sweetheart." Meadow reassured her. "We can still have fun."

"Fun?" The Bride wept. "My best friend just got blown up on a jet ski!"

"Best friend?" Liv butted in. "Didn't you tell her to like fuck off?"

"I thought I was your best friend." Meadow whined.

"Now is not the time for semantics, Liv," said the Bride. "We don't speak ill of the dead." The Bride pulled slime out of her hair and held it up like a used condom. "What even is this shit? How is it still in my hair?"

"Come on girl, let's get you to your room, you've said all you can say to the police." Meadow took her by the shoulder.

"Neon thirst trap?" The Bride asked.

"Wait, you still want to go out after all that's happened?" Bart was flabbergasted.

"I still want to go out!" Andre raised his hand.

"We can go to the hospital with her remains." Liv suggested. "And wait for her family."

"The hospital? The bitch is dead, try the morgue." Joked Heather in bad taste.

"And me?" The Bride was nearly feral. "What about me Liv, look at me!"

Liv had something to say but let it pass.

"Listen sweety, we've done all we can do for Brazil, but she's gone." Meadow continued. "What we need to do is support our Bride-to-be."

"Yeah." The Bride went on. "I think I knew Brazil better than any of us, and if I can speak for her? More than anything Brazil loved to party."

"Do you have any words to share for her passing?" Andre asked.

"Well, Brazil would not have wanted us to go to the hospital... or the morgue, no. Brazil would have wanted us to go to Señor Frog's."

"Yes!" Andre cheered. "To celebrate her life!"

"And fucked up and get great content!" Screamed Emily A and the 'party' cheered.

"She was so amazing."

"One of a kind."

"Didn't she like sue her great aunt for defamation or something?" asked Heather.

"No, idiot, that was me. I'm suing my gynecologist." Emily B said and the police investigator noted it down.

"TMI, Emily?" Meadow was disgusted.

"Not like that sicko!" Emily B continued. "I'm not deformed or anything. So I missed a few copays and the doctor's office sent the bill to collections. They royally screwed my credit score! Luckily my mom's an attorney and we are taking his office for what it's worth." The police investigator crossed that out.

"Brazil did sue her aunt though." Tanya added. "She was no saint."

"Yes!" Emily A butt in. "I know the whole story."

"She sued her aunt?" The Bride asked. "I didn't know that-"

"Take this down." Emily A ordered the police investigator and he scribbled. "Brazil sued her aunt out of her home for cash."

"What the actual fuck are we talking about here?" Liv was shocked. "She just blew up on a jet ski? What does this have to do with anything?"

Emily A was disgusted. "It could be like evidence or something."

"Moral of the story officer-" said the Bride. "Is that Brazil would have wanted us to party in her name."

"Amen." Andre gave a sigh of relief and the police investigator slapped closed his notepad. Liv's face glowed in horror with the whites and reds and blues of the police lights.

XIV

CLUBBED TO DEATH

White lights, red lights, blue lights flashed in the nightclub. The light chopped Liv's face into blocks of color. Bass heavy music punched through bodies like a panic attack. The bachelorette party danced, all of them neon drunk. The Bride stood out in the crowd. A white top with her neon sash looking for attention. She was a glowing mistake ready to happen.

"Drinks are so expensive here!" Heather complained.

"Follow me." Emily A grabbed her arm. "Let me show you how it's done."

In the back of the club at a VIP table in the shadows, Miguel and his Quintana Roo Cartel cronies were holed up. Miguel drank a tall cold beer. He wore an elegant slim fit two-piece suit.

"So, Miguel?" A soldier asked him leaning in. "You've been at that resort all day, you scope out an operative yet? Find anything interesting?"

"You didn't hear?" Another soldier butted in. "All the police today? Scanner and radios were going off about some sort of explosion."

"Just some freak accident." Miguel watched the bachelorette party dance under the moving lights. "A girl blew herself up on a faulty jet ski. Nothing more, nothing less."

"A fucking jet ski? Unbelievable."

Miguel couldn't care less about this conversation. All he cared about was the black haired beauty on the dance floor: Becky. She was dancing with her friends and he watched her. She hadn't seen him, not yet. He was waiting. He was absolutely enamored with her beauty. A soldier snapped his fingers in front of Miguel's face and snapped him out of his trance.

"I said, what else did you find Miguel? Any feds?"

"Nothing. Absolutely nothing." Miguel finished his drink. "If the feds were there, I would have found them. There's nothing at the hotel but bachelorette parties, spring breakers, drunks and retirees."

Behind the bar a suspicious waiter tilted a yellow dropper over three cocktails, slow, deliberate, poisonous. "Gentlemen." The suspicious waiter arrived at the Cartel's VIP table with the three poisoned drinks balanced like sin. "Drinks are on the house." The waiter handed out the drinks to the cartel men. Miguel reached for a poisoned drink right as Emily A and hobbling Heather crash landed at their table.

"Hi Boys!" Emily A chirped. "My friend here thinks you're cute!"

"Hi ladies. Oh, does she?" A soldier laughed.

"Sooooo, which of you gentlemen wants to buy us single ladies a drink?" Heather hobbled right into the suspicious waiter and knocked over two of the poisoned drinks. With a crash and a splash they spilled on the floor and on the table.

"Careful! Idiot!" The waiter accosted her.

"That's no way to speak to a lady!" Miguel was firm. "Especially not ones as beautiful as these two." Miguel handed the still intact poisoned cocktail to Emily A, as smooth as the devil.

"How about a goddamn refill!" Demanded a soldier and he slammed his hand onto the wet table. "We're thirsty! This is only one drink for these two ladies."

"That's ok." Emily A smiled, innocent and drunk. "We can share! So do you want to dance with us?"

The Quintana Roo soldier looked back at the others with a fat drunk smile and followed Emily A to the dance floor. Heather hobbled after her, grabbed the poisoned drink out of her hand and tilted the glass to her lips to drink. Meadow was there just in time to save the day, ripping the poison away from her like a magician with a grudge.

"I think you have had enough sweety." Meadow said, pulling Emily A away from the soldier. "Dancing with the locals, what are you crazy?"

"He was so cute." Emily A pouted.

The soldier stood on the dance floor alone and despondent. Nearby Bart pulled Liv into the light and the music. "Come on, let's live a little." He said and they danced.

The poison cocktail made it's rounds amongst the group like a bad rumor, from bridesmaid to bridesmaid. Everyone too drunk to have it, too distracted to care. The glass was set down, moved around, knocked over nearly spilling and picked up again and again until it ended up in Liv's hands.

"Cheers!" Bart held up his glass to hers.

"Cheers." Liv said, lifting the poisoned drink to her lips, but Meadow bumped into her mid dance unknowingly saving the day for the second time.

"Hello, Liv. Having fun?"

Liv lowered the poisoned drink having never taken a sip. "Yea. Trying to."

"Today was crazy. This is crazy." Meadow kept dancing. Liv slowed.

"Right? Thank you for saying that."

"But we do it for her." Meadow pointed her chin toward the Bride. The Bride was drunker than humanly possible. She was drunker than anyone else in that room. She laughed at an empty shot glass and demanded another from a bartender who wasn't there.

"She's one of a kind." Remarked Liv.

"That she is and so am I." The music changed and Meadow changed up her dancing, faster now, breathing every word hot into Liv's ear, shouting over the beat. "It takes merit to be the maid of honor. Not just luck from some childhood pact."

"Yeah ok." Liv stopped dancing.

"I want it. Let me have it." Meadow continued. "You may be t maid of honor on paper, but everyone knows I'm the maid of honor de facto. Get it?"

"I'm happy to share the title with you." Liv was static in a swaying dancing crowd. She wanted to play peacemaker and get along to be along. "We can just ask-"

"I don't ask and I don't share." Meadow flipped her hair back. "I get what I want."

Liv was done. She set the poisoned drink down on a table and walked away, Bart followed her out the door.

XV

UNDERBOSSED GETS OVERSAUCED

The Quintana Roo soldier was back at the table after striking out with Heather. "Struck out?" Miguel smirked.

"Cockblocked by some bitch." He shook his head. That's when the beefy tatted up Underboss of the Quintana Roo arrived at the table. He was a bigger and flashier presence than all of the soldiers and Miguel combined. His suit was pastel and freshly ironed. His watch cost more than most people's cars. He sat with them with gravitas.

"What did I miss?" The Underboss asked. "Did I hear you struck out on some tail again?" He laughed.

"Yea, yea."

Meadow came waltzing up to the table with the poisoned cocktail in her hand, still untouched. "Hi boys." She smiled like a cheerleader holding back a dirty secret. "Thanks for buying a girl a drink. I just wanted to return the favor!"

The Underboss grabbed the poisoned drink like it owed him money. "Thank you! I'll show you boys how it's done." And he downed it without blinking, without thinking. "That's how you do it! And what's your name, beautiful?" He asked her.

"Um... Sarah." Meadow lied and away she went laughing and disappearing into a crowd. The cartel laughed too.

Miguel shook his head. "If her name is Sarah, then my name is John Smith."

At the door, the drunk Bride collapsed against Bart and Andre. Meadow herded the rest of the drunk bridesmaids out of the club like loose cattle. The wasted Bride giggled, barely standing up. Bart fought her white veil stuck to his face. "Come on girls!" Meadow took charge. "Cabs are here, let's go!" And the bachelorette party stumbled out of the club.

Just before she was pulled out of the club, Becky locked eyes with Miguel long enough for it to matter. Both wondered if this was what true love felt like. But Meadow was pulling her away before Becky could act on it.

"There goes your opportunity." The Underboss joked to Miguel.

"Where's that waiter?" Miguel asked. "I'm thirsty."

Outside, the line at the club snaked around the block. Music leaked from the doors. The town pulsed. Traffic lights in the heat. Honking cars and motorbikes. Liv stood, taking in the outside air. The Bride got sick between two parked cars. Andre dropped the Bride's arm and bummed a cigarette from some hot stranger, leaving Bart to deal with the vomit. "A little help here?" Bart called out to Liv. Liv pulled the Bride upright and the girls shuffled into cabs.

"Don't worry I've got you." Liv comforted the sick Bride.

The Bride stank of vomit and cheap perfume. Her head wound pulsated like a beating heart. It was brutally infected. The slime pool had done her dirty. A rash was crawling up her neck like a slow curse, decaying in real time. She smiled. "I'm so sorry I got a little tipsy girlies. I'll have the whole trip to make it up to you, I promise."

"We've got you girl." Meadow rallied the team. "Liv you're with us. Bart you take the next cab."

The Bride leaned in to Bart and kissed him on his cheek, leaving vomit on his chin stubble like a parting gift. "Thank you Andre. You are the best gay best friend a girl could ask for."

"You're welcome." Bart sighed and the Bride's cab took off leaving him in the dust. Bart stood there staring. Andre was chatting up a storm with a local cutie and smoking his cigarette. "Really ditched me there." Bart said to Andre.

"Sorry bitch." Andre blew cigarette smoke into Bart's face. Not a care in the world.

Back in the nightclub a fresh waiter brought a fresh round of drinks for the Quintana Roo Cartel men at VIP. The Underboss laughed and drank. Miguel sat watching the crowd like a hawk looking for a meal. The soldiers joked amongst each other, all of them trying to impress the other. The club spun.

"So, we've got nothing more to worry about then." The Underboss said. "Maybe it's all just been one big distraction."

"Could be." Miguel commented.

"Then I say we get Boss Antonio to OK us moving on the Familia Yucatán now." A soldier argued. "We finish them off. The Feds can wait."

"Boss wants us to hang low, we hang low." Miguel said.

"We hit them. " The Underboss coughed. "We hit them hard in the jungle and we end this-" His coughing was fierce.

"You okay boss?" A soldier asked.

The Underboss stood, coughing uncontrollably now. Then he choked and fell like a dead weight, right on the hard concrete ground. He was seizing and vomiting blood all over the place. Eyes bulging, face purpling.

"Somebody call an ambulance!" A soldier screamed but the Underboss went stiff, cold and dead. "He's dead." A soldier checked for a pulse.

"Then do CPR, dammit!"

"Stop." Miguel's voice was flat. "He was poisoned. You touch him, you're dead too."

"It was that bitch then! 'Sarah' she poisoned him. She's dead! Dead!"

"Her?" Miguel shook his head. "Couldn't have been. She was just some drunk girl."

"It's like the boss said," A soldier reflected. "These Feds, these operatives and assassins could be anyone. Vixens! Highly trained!"

Miguel sat back in his seat. "If not her, then who?"

XVI

WHO, WHAT, WHERE AND WHY YUCATÁN?

The suspicious waiter suspiciously hauled ass out of the city and down a main road. He drove like a mad man in his beat up truck. The engine screamed, gravel spit. He ripped off his clip on bow tie and pulled off his fake mustache and prosthetic nose from sweaty skin. He tossed the fake nose out the window. Marco was the name his mother had gave him. Marco made a sharp left off the main drag, tires screaming onto a dirt road, headlights flashing in dust into a dark jungle that swallowed him whole.

Deep in that jungle was the Familia Yucatán Cartel's compound. They were the sworn enemies of the Quintana Roo Cartel. At the compound, Yucatán soldiers stuffed pipe bombs, loaded 5.56 rounds into old magazines. Torchlight made their malnourished faces look demonic. Workers boiled coca leaves, clouds of steam rose up over cookfires like old angry spirits.

Hardened and war weathered Boss Francisco stood over a batch of finished cocaine. His army fatigues were caked with dirt and old sweat. He snorted a tester, winced, sneezed and smiled like a lunatic. "Woo! Good stuff!" He was overjoyed with the product and grabbed the neck of a soldier and walked with him down the camp. The heat of the jungle stuck to their backs. "Perfect. We will do well here. And what's the big deal? So, we spend a couple of weeks in this jungle compound. It could be worse you know! We could have had our cocks cut off and shoved down our throats or up our asses. No, no, no! Look at this place! We have it made! Paradise. We just keep making product, keep making money, keep staying alive. It's like camping!"

"But how much longer, boss?" The soldier kicked the dirt. "I haven't seen my family in weeks. They probably think I'm dead."

"It's good if they think you're dead! It keeps them alive." Boss Francisco clapped the soldier on the back like they were best buds. "You're my number one man. You want us to stay alive? Then play dead! And when this all blows over you can surprise your family by being alive! How fun does that sound?"

Headlights of Marco's old truck slashed through the camp and the truck rattled to a stop. Marco hopped out.

"Marco!" Boss Francisco embraced him. "How'd you make out on your assignment?"

"Failed sir." Marco had his head down. "I'm sorry."

"It's ok." Boss Francisco held him close, like forgiveness, like love. Then he kneed him square in the balls. Knockout. Marco dropped, folding like paper, gasping and gurgling. "You're weak!" Boss Francisco spat. "And that's why we're still out here in this jungle! In this shit!"

"I thought you said it's paradise, boss? Like camping?" A soldier asked.

"I hate camping." Boss Francisco turned with a voice deadly and placed his heavy booted foot on Marco's throat. His phone rang, he answered. "Hello?" And his face lit up like it was Christmas morning. He laughed and pulled his boot off of Marco who coughed. "Good. Yes. Amazing. Goodbye. Bye bye!" He hung up with a heavy smile and lifted Marco to his feet. "Sorry about that Marco. My emotions get the best of me sometimes. But you know what I always say. Strength is everything! Power. As the boss I had to show a little strength. But I'm ok now. It's all ok."

"What was that call, boss?" Marco coughed.

"I just received some very good news. Your target was that Lieutenant Miguel, right? And a couple no name soldiers?"

Marco nodded, still gasping.

"Well, it looks like Boss Antonio's Underboss met their sticky end tonight. Kill confirmed."

"How?" Marco asked, confused. "When I left I-"

"Did I say it was you?" Boss Francisco snapped. "No, better than you. The United States CIA. The rumors are true. They are sending highly trained killers here. And they are working on our behalf. My source on the inside says they'll send supplies, money, backup, anything to keep this war going, anything to justify their wages. If I were you, I'd watch the skies for air drops. They know where we are." And with that Boss Francisco walked off laughing, high on cocaine, gunpowder and paranoia.

XVII

DEMOTION PROMOTION

The next miserable morning the sun was already hot and heavy overhead. At the resort the pool chlorine was so thick in the air it was like war gas. A hazmat team stood around the slime pool, emptying it out, cleaning it up and taking samples in vials like it was a murder scene. The hazmat techs wore yellow suits and gas masks, rubber boots. Their oxygen tanks hissed like angry snakes. One hazmat tech waved a Geiger counter over a bubbling slime sample. It clicked and kept clicking. Not a good sign. Another tech scooped the sludge into more test tubes. Whatever that living slime was and whatever it was rapidly mutating into was uncharted territory for the scientific community.

The morning sun hit like regret for the decaying Bride in her room. She slugged back three Advil and chased it with Gatorade mixed with surprise tequila. The tequila nearly made her sick. She looked at her horrid reflection. Her eyes were like a doll's eyes. She was pale except for the red rash that was spreading fast up her neck. She figured it was nothing a little makeup couldn't fix. She was wrong. Her head wound pulsated. It was cracked, wet and stanky. Her fingertips found the rash and trailed it down her neck to her back. It was like spilled bubbly paint. Should she go to a doctor? Yes. Would she go to the doctor and threaten ruining her party and her buzz? No.

She dragged a makeup brush over the clumpy rash like a lawn mower over rocks. Foundation over infection, concealer over decay. The state of her hotel room was no better than the state of her body. Like how dogs look like to their owners, her room looked and smelled like a dead dog, whatever that means. It was a crime scene staged by entitled influencers. Empty cans, torn clothes, and torn drapes. Makeup spilled all over countertops, and of course vomit in the sink.

The door was already unlocked when Liv walked in and winced at the smell. She powered through. "Hey, good morning. How are you feeling?" She asked the Bride.

"Liv my love!" The Bride got up unsteady, her arms wide and she wrapped herself around Liv like something halfway between an embrace and a biological threat. Pus from her head wound smeared onto Liv's hair like day old cream cheese over a stale bagel.

"Oh my God." Liv gagged. "You should really see a doctor. Maybe they have an urgent care at the resort."

"What? This?" The Bride pat down the leak at the side of her head with paper towel. "This is fine! No big deal! It's this hangover that's truly killing me."

Liv was sick and pressed a hand to her cramping stomach, sore, silent and miserable. "Maybe if you ate something instead?"

The Bride grabbed an open beverage and took a swig. Deliciously disgusting. "Yeah, yeah. Meadow brought me food already. But I couldn't keep anything down." The Bride gestured to a paper plate on the nightstand half full of old food. A sad sunny side up egg, limp dick bacon, cold potatoes and shriveled up toast that had her sad fiancé's face toasted on top of it. "She's such a sweetheart I swear. Isn't she? My Meadow."

Liv's eyes lingered on the plate. A house fly landed on the toast and died. "Yea. She's one of a kind."

"That's what I always say!" The Bride beamed.

Liv cleared her throat. "So, what's up? Meadow said you wanted to talk to me about something?"

Silence and the Bride patted the bed, a threatening invitation disguised as comfort. Liv sat, hesitantly.

"I'm sorry... I." The Bride started and hesitated.

"No. I'm sorry." Liv cut in. "I'm sorry if I've been disconnected. Distant. I know a lot is expected from the maid of honor. Maybe I'm not maid of honor material. Maybe. But I'm going to be. I'll be better. I've had a lot going on back home, things I want to tell you but don't know if I can yet." Liv winced and pressed her abdomen.

"No, Liv." The Bride jumped in with faux words and sticky insincerity. "I'm sorry too. I'm sorry if I've been disconnected. If I've been distant. If I've been cold. I just drank too much last night is all... I don't know what got into me." She laughed an awful sickly laugh.

"Well, it's your party."

"I know. And that's why I'm so happy you're here! You're so real. Like, I've known you since day one. All the other girlies, I love them yes, but most of them I met in college and that's just like something you can't totally trust. You know what I mean? Because we were always so drunk or high together. That's all it took to be friends with them. I mean they're all so boring sober!"

"Well maybe we can take it easy together on this trip. We can have fun together. We don't have to get so fucked up. We don't have to drink so much, maybe."

The Bride laughed, dry and bitter. She needed another drink. She stared down Liv with dead eyes. "I don't think so. I don't know what to do with these girlies except drink. Sometimes I just... I put up a wall, you know? And I don't know why but in the past, I've just burned so many bridges. Not again. I don't want to lose my girlfriends. I don't want to lose you." She took Liv's hand and held it tight like it meant something.

"What about Brazil? I-"

The Bride dropped Liv's hand like it was a dead fish. She instantly changed her mood for the worse. She was disgusted. "There's something else. We need to talk."

"We are talking..."

"Then listen." The Bride regurgitated a large farty breath. "It's not working. You on the plane. You and Brazil. The club. The dinner. Everything."

"Okay."

"I love you Liv, you know that." The Bride stood, hobbled a bit and paced back and forth. "But let's face it... You are just not maid of honor material. Pact or not."

The words hit Liv like a swarm of mosquitoes at dusk on a hot July day when you just found out your boyfriend is cheating on you with that hot fucker that sits behind you in third period calculus. Inevitably specific and annoying. Liv's heart sank, and she swallowed on a suddenly dry throat. So loud the Bride could hear it.

"No, no, no!" The Bride consoled her to her chagrin. "Don't think of it as a demotion. Think of it as an opportunity! I love you Liv! You know that. You have time now. Time to do what you want. Time to enjoy this trip and not think so much about all this silly maid of honor stuff. Meadow can take care of everything for me. For us. Ok?" The Bride's words bit like that metaphorical swarm of mosquitoes.

Liv couldn't believe it. The Bride spoke like it was a group decision, like they had voted on it. Liv was speechless. There was a knock at the already ajar door and in stepped the new maid of honor: the terribly mischievous Meadow. She smiled like a chimp at the zoo, playful yet dangerous. "I'm not interrupting anything, am I?" She asked with insincere sincerity. Heather hobbled in just behind her, a smug grin on her pudgy face.

"Meadow! Heather!" The Bride called to them. "No, no, come in, come in."

Liv swallowed her pride. "I'll get going then."

"No! You can stay." The Bride's voice said one thing with a tone that said another.

"It's alright. I'll get going."

"Giddy-up." Heather joked.

"Alright then, well get ready. Naughty and Nautical! We'll see you on the boat!"

Liv said nothing. She smiled at a corner of her dry lips. They cracked in the Mexican heat. She left.

Meadow stepped on past her to join the bride, all victorious and pompous. "How'd she take the news?" She asked the Bride once Liv had cleared the room.

The Bride didn't miss a beat. "If she wanted it... she would have fought for it."

Meadow smirked, like a sadistic babysitter who just kicked a toddler in the groin. She had won for now.

XVIII

TO BE, OR NOT TO BE:
THAT'S THE ANNOYING QUESTION

Sanguine Rose frolicked at the beach like a kid from the arctic who had never experienced the warmth of day. Sand kicked up behind her like she was the Road Runner. She wore the same clothes as she had yesterday and why not? Neon thirst trap doesn't go out of style so quickly in Tulum. The waters of the Caribbean Ocean would give her a salty wash and rinse cycle. She smelled of salt, sweat, tequila and marijuana. She hummed something strange and familiar, half a melody and half a hallucination.

Out on the water a swarm of toys for rich kids flew on by. Sailboats and jet skis cutting foam. A couple was parasailing and was reeled back in like a caught fish. By cosmic circumstance a coconut vendor appeared in front of Sanguine Rose like a desert mirage. Thirsty, Sanguine Rose dug through her hemp-sewn sling bag. She sorted through gummies, loose pills, little baggies, and found the cash she was looking for, stained with melted chocolate. She looked back and forth from the coconut vendor to the parasailing boat. It looked like so much fun she thought. What should she buy, what a dilemma.

Back on the dock the parasail attendants struggled with an old harness stuck to the boat. A buckle on the harness bent, one carabiner strained and stretched and broke free. No one noticed the damage. No one cared.

Liv packed her bags quickly, determined to erase herself from this fumbled shitshow. She figured if she left now they'd all soon forget about her. She was committed to forgetting them too. It wouldn't be easy, but she could do it. She hoped she could do it. Bart came into their hotel room like it was another normal day. "Getting your outfit together?" He asked her. "Naughty and Nautical?"

"No." She held back tears. "I'm leaving."

Bart took a step closer. "What are you talking about? What's wrong? I thought we decided last night we'd stick it out?"

"She demoted me, Bart. She made Meadow the maid of honor."

"What a relief!" Bart sighed.

"No. It's fucked up!" Liv collapsed onto a pile of loos clothes, her head in her hands.

Bart sat next to her and placed his hairy arm over her soft shoulder. "Well, she's fucked up. It figures she'd pull some shit like this."

"Yeah."

"So did you book a flight home yet?"

"No." Liv started packing again. "I don't even know what I'm doing..."

"I have an idea. Why don't we get some fresh air? Go for a walk?"

"I just need time to myself."

"Alright, I'm here if you need me girl."

"A walk on the beach sounds nice. Clear my head. That's it."

Bart got up and threw on a cheap sailor's hat like he was in a theme park commercial.

"But you'll be back for the boat." He said sternly. "Fuck all those bitches and fuck what they think. Don't leave me to fend for myself. Deal?"

"Deal."

XIX

CLOSE ENCOUNTERS

Miguel of the Quintana Roo Cartel pushed a bell cart down a hallway in the resort. He was a good actor and blended in, playing the part. He had to do it like the CIA. If they were undercover, then so was he. Every guest was a suspect to him. Were they FBI? CIA? DEA? Or just plain old tourists. He wasn't so sure, but he was there to find out. His phone buzzed, a text message from Boss Antonio glowing like a cryptic warning.

"I said I'll be right there!" Beautiful Becky rounded the corner in that hallway. She was dolled up in her sluttiest sailor outfit. "Hold the elevator for me. I forgot my sunglasses!" Her sunglasses were perched right on top of her silly slutty head.

Miguel looked up and the two would-be lovers collided. Becky's sunglasses dropped to the floor, slow motion like. Both of them froze in time. In an instant they were smitten. Love was their destiny.

"Hello." Miguel greeted her. His words caressed her like smooth velvet on naked skin.

"Hi," said the ever bashful Becky. They both bent down for the sunglasses. Hands touched. Skin to skin. Static electricity. Hairs stood at the back of their necks. Miguel took the glasses and handed them to Becky.

"Are these yours?" He asked.

"How did you know?" She blushed.

"I have a way with knowing things. What's your name, mi amor?"

The Emilys and Tanya rounded the corner like a Greek tragedy. "Becky come on let's get moving! You can have my sunglasses." Emily B stopped and stared at the handsome Miguel and was taken aback. "Oh, hello there."

"Aren't you going to introduce us to your friend?" Tanya asked Becky smiling.

Becky blushed. "Well, I haven't even introduced myself. I'm Becky." She held a out a hand for a handshake. Miguel squared his shoulders, never taking his eyes off of her. He grabbed her hand and kissed it so softly she could melt.

"Becky." He said with warmth enough to melt butter. "It's a pleasure to meet you. They call me Miguel." His voice had bravado as thick as melted dark chocolate and all the girls in that hallway could feel his passion. Becky glanced at Miguel's name tag. It read 'Ronaldo.' Miguel caught her shifting eyes. "Oh this. Yes uh... Ronaldo is my nickname."

"Well alright Miguel Ronaldo." Becky gave him a wink and a sultry smile.

The Bride, Meadow, and hobbling Heather rounded the hallway giggling and stumbling. "Come on girls let's get moving." The Bride placed an unwanted hand on Miguel. "And sir, if we can have room 237 serviced pronto! It's a total warzone in there. Alright girls, let's hit it."

Meadow grabbed Becky and pulled her to the elevator. One last lingering glance at Miguel, both of them smitten. Both of them in love.

XX

A DATE WITH DESTINY

Sanguine Rose twirled in the sand. She balanced two coconut drinks in her hands. On the beach Liv sat idly staring at the surf. "Liv!" Sanguine Rose shouted when she spotted her.

"Oh. Hi Sanguine Rose." Liv greeted her dejected.

"This is so perfect! What a beautiful day!" Sanguine Rose offered a coconut drink to Liv. "I was looking for someone to share these with. You want?"

"No thanks."

"Mind if I join you?"

"No offense... but I'd rather be alone."

"None taken." Sanguine Rose began to walk away and looked back, a gleam of destiny in her eyes.

"That was rude." Liv muttered, thirsty now. "Sure. Come sit with me."

Sanguine Rose plopped down next to Liv and dropped the drink right into Liv's lap like a bowling ball. "Enjoy!"

"Jesus." The drink spilled on her, but then she had some. Delicious.

"What are you up to?"

"Well, I went for a walk to clear my head. Didn't work. Just noise."

"I'm with you on that. Sometimes it's all too much to handle you know?"

"I keep letting people run all over me." Liv sighed. "I expect them to change but they never do. Fuck me... I just want to fuck off and get as far away from this place and as far away from these people as possible. No offense to you."

Sanguine Rose grinned. "You look like you could use a little pick me up. Cheers!" She clinked coconuts and drank deep.

"Damn this is good." Liv drank more. "You didn't drug this did you?"

"God no... Do you want me to?"

"No... I mean I don't think so."

"I think you need something extra. How about an adventure?" Sanguine Rose looked at the surf and right on cue a boat attendant walked up to the two twenty-somethings. Life vests and waivers in hand.

"Hi miss. We're ready for you." The attendant said.

"What's this?" Liv asked.

"I booked parasailing for two. I didn't know who my plus one would be but now it's you. I think it's meant to be. It's our destiny."

"We're supposed to be on a boat with the Bride in less than an hour."

"That was today? Well, then we'll make it a quick adventure, right sir? Two boat rides are better than one."

"Whatever you'd like, miss."

Liv stared at the life jackets and the waivers. Then grabbed them both like grabbing fate by the balls.

Back inside the resort Bart stepped out of his room and into a long hallway. His sailor costume was cringey as fuck. Andre was there, waiting to go into his room. "Hey." Bart said as weak as a salted slug. He wouldn't even make eye contact.

"Hey yourself."

"Yeah, I'll see you at the boat." Bart kept walking, turned back when a surge of confidence hit him. "Do you not like me or something?"

Andre shrugged. "I like my alone time. Sharing a room kinda sucks."

"Well getting cigarette smoke blown in your face after getting vomited on kinda sucks."

"Well you kinda suck."

"Well you just suck!" Bart shouted.

"You would know. Sucks to suck." And with that Andre slammed the door on Bart's face.

XXI

BRB FYI CIA

"This is amazing!" Sanguine Rose shouted over the wind and threw up her arms. "Look ma, no hands!" She and Liv were flying high over the ocean. They were parasailing 50 feet above the water but to Liv it might as well have been 500 feet. Wind screaming, rope straining, parachute flailing.

"I'm gonna throw up!" Liv screamed holding tight to the harness. "Then I'm gonna shit my pants!"

"Woo! Oh yeah!" Sanguine Rose was in heaven. She was completely oblivious of the imminent danger. The harness holding them to the boat twisted and turned, metal whined and sheared. Carabiner threads snapped like twisted tendons.

"Look down!" Liv saw the disaster in waiting.

Sanguine Rose looked out to the view. "I know! It's beautiful! You can see the city from here! It's just a speck. Oh, what magic! Oh my God and look at all this jungle! Have you ever felt so free?"

"No! The rope! Look at the rope!" Liv's panic cut through the wind and Sanguine Rose's joy. "It's breaking! The... The thing. I don't know what it's called."

"The boat? Did you forget the word boat, Liv? You are so silly!"

"No! Our harness! The carabiner! It's breaking! It's breaking! WE'RE GONNA FUCKING DIE!"

"Oh carabiner. Yeah, that's a tricky one! Oh shit, there it goes."

SNAP! The carabiner split in two and the cable attaching them to the boat fell like a limp dick into the sea. The boat sped off like it was ready to pick up another customer. Cash paid, see you later Liv and Sanguine Rose.

"We're FUCKED!" Liv screamed.

"We're FREE!" Sanguine Rose shouted in joy and a gust of wind caught them and lifted them higher and higher to 500 feet but to Liv it might as well have been 5,000 feet.

"Oh no. Oh no. Oh no." Farther and farther they went up and over the jungle.

"It's fine!" Sanguine Rose reassured her with intoxicated confidence. "The wind's got us! We'll just coast back to the beach!"

Liv's voice broke. "Look around! There's no beach left! No resort! Just jungle!"

"We're fine..." Sanguine Rose squinted. "Hey... How do you steer this thing?"

XXII

A GIFT FROM ABOVE

Deep in the jungle the Familia Yucatán plotted their next move. Their options were limited, and team morale was at an all-time low. Soldiers played cards and chewed coca leaves. They spit and drank warm cola. One of them had jerry rigged a car battery to an old CRT TV that played the Wizard of Oz on VHS. A rough looking soldier polished his rifle, held it up. It gleamed in the sunlight. A shadow flashed, and he saw the silhouette of a parachute gliding over the jungle, quickly hidden behind the trees now.

"Boss! Boss!" He yelled running to Boss Francisco's tent.

"What?" Boss Francisco rose from an old, tired cot. He pulled a long revolver from under his pillow and aimed it at the soldier. "Can't you see I'm napping? I need my naps!" He held the revolver so limp you'd think he'd drop it. He inspected a half drunken bottle of tequila, thinking about taking another sip. He did.

"Boss! You told us tell you if we saw anything! I think it's an airdrop sir."

"Oh shit." Francisco dropped the bottle and stumbled out of the tent barefoot. His troops were scrambling, pointing to the sky. "Which way was the airdrop?"

"That way, sir!" A soldier pointed.

"No, it was that way!" Another soldier argued. They all got their directions criss-cross apple sauced.

"Look! There!" Boss Francisco caught a glimpse of the gliding parachute. He was elated. "What did I say boys?" Francisco grinned wide. "I knew the CIA would come."

"I got a good look at it, boss." A soldier reflected. "It wasn't a crate. It was two people."

"Two operatives then! Were they armed?"

"Hard to tell. They were far away."

"Well let's get going then. No time to waste." Boss Francisco dressed fast. "We covered this jungle with booby traps. If we don't warn those operatives they'll end up blowing themselves up."

"How do we know they're here to help us... And not here to kill us?" Marco asked with a low flat voice.

"Well we'll have to find out for ourselves. We have the advantage either way. The jungle is ours."

"Holy fuck!" Liv screamed gliding low over the jungle canopy, close enough her flip flops clipped the tip tops of the treetops. "Holy fucking fuck!"

"This is amazing!" Sanguine Rose laughed like a lunatic, not a care in the world.

"We're dead! We're fucking dead!"

Leaves slapped their ankles. Branches reached up their legs and grabbed for their faces. Leaves clipped the lines of their parachute. So close to death they were and then at the last possible moment the jungle opened up to a sunlit glade, green and wide and welcoming. Lucky as all hell they landed in soft grass with a slump and a hard stop.

"That was awesome!" Sanguine Rose spit dirt and played with the limp parachute like a cape.

Liv crawled from underneath the rainbow parachute, body shaking. "We're dead. We're dead."

"We're alive!" Sanguine Rose was elated.

"We're in the middle of a fucking jungle in the middle of fucking nowhere!" Liv kicked off the parachute.

"And that is exactly where you wanted to be a half hour ago, remember?" Sanguine Rose winked.

"I guess I best be careful what I wish for." Liv wiped dirt from her face.

"There's a road around here somewhere." Sanguine Rose peered around like she knew the place already. "This ain't my first time lost in a jungle, Liv. Follow me."

XXIII

AHOY MATEY

Back at the resort the bachelorette party gathered at the docks. They lined up impatiently for their yacht party day. The party boat was ugly as sin. Not so much a yacht as it was an overpriced mistake. The girls were all naughty and nautical themed and screaming.

"Let's get a move on!" The Bride jeered. She was melting in the heat. Literally melting. The toxins from the booze and the slime pool rushed through her bloodstream. She looked like death covered in makeup. Her 'friends' whispered amongst themselves that maybe, no definitely she should go to the hospital. Or at the very least see the cosmetologist at the resort spa. But no one dared tell her that. No one dared to say anything negative to the Bride at her own party.

"We're ready for you." The captain of the party boat said.

"Alright everyone, let's go!" Meadow clapped her hands taking charge.

Attendants helped load the drunk girls and boys onto the ugly party boat. The girls were all too much glitter, too little clothing and too much noise. Coolers cracked open, seltzers popped. The attendants served appetizers that the girlies called appeteasers.

"Hold off on the drinks, ladies!" The Bride jeered grinning. "I have something even better. But keep it on the DL."

"What is it?" Tanya asked.

"It's the goods from Sanguine Rose." The Bride dug into her purse. "Where is she even anyway?"

"I think I saw her pocketing some grapes and ketchup packets at breakfast." Heather shrugged. "Haven't seen her since."

"Take one each." The Bride flashed her bag of psychedelic brownies. "Just a small piece is all you need."

"What's in these?" Emily A asked swallowing one whole.

"They're psychedelic mushroom brownies! I've already had mine and I think I'm starting to feel it. God I hope it cures this hangover. My head is killing me!"

"Don't mind if I do." Andre grabbed one and down the hatch it went.

"This is gonna be the best day of our lives girlies!" More and more of them grabbed psychedelic brownie pieces and ate.

"Oh my god these are delicious!"

Nobody asked questions. Questions are for nerds.

"Alright let's go!" Meadow screamed at the captain swallowing her psychedelic brownie. Attendants untied the boat from the dock.

"Wait, where's Liv?" Becky asked.

"Missing." Meadow muttered. "That comes as no surprise."

"What do you mean by that?" Becky asked.

"Oh nothing."

"And Sanguine Rose isn't here either. We should wait for her at least?"

"Obviously yes we are waiting for them." Bart insisted, worried about his friend.

"And waste our precious time?" Andre waved him off. "I don't think so."

"Sanguine Rose does her own thing." The Bride said. "Her absence comes as no surprise."

Heather laughed. "I bet you she didn't even know this was on the schedule."

"But Liv? We should wait for your maid of honor." Becky said worried, but the boat's crew kept untethering the boat.

"Hold on." Bart pulled out his phone. "I'll call her. She said she was going for a walk to clear her head. I'm sure she's right behind us."

"Alright everyone." The Bride made an announcement to the group. "I guess now is as good a time as ever. I have an announcement to make." She announced.

"No, no!" Meadow jumped in. "Make it a toast. Captain, can we get some champagne please?"

The boat attendants uncorked a bottle and handed out champagne flutes. The boat freely drifted away from the dock.

The Bride raised her glass. "Everyone... I have made Meadow here my new maid of honor."

"Yay!" Heather squealed like a piggy.

"Wait what? Why?" Becky asked surprised.

"Well. Meadow fits the role."

Meadow lifted her glass like a prom queen accepting her crown. "Come on ladies! Raise your glasses. This will be the wedding of the century!"

Bart rejected a champagne flute and glanced down at his phone. "She's not picking up."

"Alright, so a bitch got fired." Andre laughed. "No way she's showing her face now. Full throttle captain! Or set sail, whatever they say. Yippie ki-yay! Wide open waters here I cum!"

The boat pulled away. Bart called Liv again, but it went straight to voicemail. The beach looked back at him like a distant friend.

"I'm sorry about your friend." Becky consoled Bart.

"It's alright." Bart lied to himself. "She's probably sitting pretty with a Mai Tai right about now."

XXIV

BOATS AND HOES

Deep in that Mexican jungle, Liv and Sanguine Rose trudged on, sweat soaked, bug bitten and dehydrated. Mosquitoes swarmed them like one thousand tiny knives. Liv slapped one of the fuckers when it bit her neck.

"So if you met a genie." Sanguine Rose asked her nearly out of breath, "and you had three wishes... what would they be?"

Liv crushed another mosquito against her leg. "Nasty fucking bloodsuckers. Are you serious? Oh, I don't know... One: Get the fuck out of this jungle. Two: Get laid. Three: Go Home."

"Wow! So humble. Usually, people wish for superpowers or money or something."

"Do you even know where you're leading us?"

"Of course girl! I used to be a Girl Scout." Sanguine squinted to the sky. "The sun sets in the west and rises in the east, so we're going..." She stopped, looked straight at the sun and blinded herself. "Ow."

"It's like noon!" Liv barked. "The sun is right above us! How are you supposed to tell direction?"

"This way." Sanguine Rose marched off like she had a clue. She didn't. And there were booby traps all around them, unseen. They walked, almost hit a tripwire. Almost triggered claymores. Almost.

Sanguine Rose kept on keeping on. "Okay, so... my three wishes. Well, first, yeah, of course get out of here. I mean

I'm having fun, but I'm getting thirsty and I'm not really vibing with the bugs."

"Oh really?"

"Second... screw it. I wanna get laid too." And she shot Liv a flirty wink. "Sounds fun!"

"Damn girl, don't look at me. You are cute and all but I don't swing that way."

"Fine." Sanguine pouted. "Third wish..."

"Go home?"

"No. I wish I could read minds. Quick- think of a number! Any number. Wait don't tell me."

Liv rolled her eyes.

"Okay I got it. Thirteen!"

"That's uncanny."

"Did I get it? Did I really get it?"

Liv slapped another mosquito on her leg. "Honestly I wasn't even thinking of a number. I was thinking about how many fucking mosquito bites I have on my left leg alone."

Sanguine dropped to her knees and started counting Liv's bug bites. "One... Two... Three-"

"Are you serious?"

"Ten, eleven, twelve, thirteen! You have thirteen bites! I knew it."

"Riveting."

Back on the party boat the bachelorette party was living the life of faux luxury. It was the polar opposite of Liv and Sanguine Rose's shituation. The bachelorette party danced the day away to shitty throwbacks. Everything on that boat was sticky, fizzy and faux. Bart kept refreshing his phone, hoping for a missed call or an unread text from Liv. Nothing.

"Come on." Becky tugged at his swim trunks almost pantsing him. "Let's dance."

"Hey! Okay, maybe in a minute. I'm just worried about Liv. Maybe she'll call."

"You get service out here? I'm sure she's fine. She probably just needs some alone time."

"Alright girlies!" Andre shouted from the boat's bar. "Shots!"

"YES!" Heather cheered.

Bart smiled to Becky. "I hope you're right."

"I know I'm right. Now dance with me." Becky grabbed his hand and dragged him away from his phone.

For Liv and Sanguine Rose it was more sweat, more dirt and no tequila shots. They just kept on trudging. A destination unknown kept their spirits up for now. "So how do you know the Bride?" Sanguine Rose asked Liv.

"She's an old friend from childhood." Liv panted.

"No way! That's so spiritual." Sanguine Rose walked right past a pit trap narrowly avoiding it. More claymores. More trip wires. More bear traps. The two walked right past death due to sheer dumb luck.

"I guess. We lived across the street growing up. Went to the same elementary school. Then my family and I moved across the country. We went our separate ways but stayed in touch. She demoted me today, you know."

"What do you mean demoted?"

"She made Meadow the maid of honor. That's why I was alone at the beach. I needed time to myself to think it over."

"Wait, I thought that annoying one was the maid of honor, what's her name?"

"Meadow." A snake pit lay ahead, hidden under some brush.

"Yes, Meadow! She's a bit... Much. So what you got demoted. So what! I think all things happen as they should. What's meant to be is meant to be." Sanguine Rose stepped on the brush and the ground collapsed. Snake pit underneath. "Oh shit!" She was falling, kicking, sliding down.

Liv was quick, grabbed Sanguine Rose's arms and dug her heels deep into the dirt. "Hold on!" and the snakes beneath them hissed, yellow and green striped with red, snapping fangs just inches from Sanguine Rose. Liv pulled hard, muscles screaming. She pulled Sanguine Rose up and out of danger and the two of them collapsed onto the jungle floor, out of breath.

"What a trip!" Sanguine Rose was laughing like a psychopath.

The party boat dropped anchor at a beautiful cove surrounded by beautiful boats full of sexy singles and one fat lard of a motherfucker who made a couple hits back in the day. Another one. Girls jumped off the boat to snorkel. The party boat's captain took a head count of girls based on life jackets. Andre jumped into the water screaming like a schoolboy. Emily B took off her life jacket and swam deep. Fish darted behind rocks to hide.

The Bride puked right over the side of the boat and no one bothered to notice except Meadow who rubbed her pimply melty back.

"Can't you do something about this rocking?" Meadow complained to the captain. "It's making our girl sick!"

"If we start moving again she'll probably feel better." The captain suggested.

"Then let's go! Girls! Back in the boat we're leaving."

One by one the girls got back on the boat and the captain counted the life jackets. The boat started up and left the cove. Out in the water, Emily B still floated snorkeling without a life jacket. She was completely oblivious. The current carried her farther and farther out. She counted fish like counting sheep.

XXV

THE GREAT BROWNIE MIX-UP

It didn't take long for the Yucatán Cartel to reach the grassy glade where Sanguine Rose and Liv had crash landed. There they found the rainbow parachute like a colorful statement. Boss Francisco slapped Marco on the back. "Good work Marco! I knew you would find it."

Marco lifted the chute. "Boss. This is just a parasailing parachute from one of the resorts. Look. It even has the resort name on it."

"Yes!" Boss Francisco was not deterred. "A perfect disguise! Hide in plain sight. Exactly what I would do if I was CIA deep undercover. Now... which way did they go?"

"Look boss!" A soldier pointed to footprints in the dirt. "Fresh tracks."

Nearby but far enough away to not get caught by the Cartel, Liv and Sanguine Rose sat in the dirt, exhausted "We should just like... sit here for a while," said Liv. "I'm toasted."

"Okay. But we should try and beat the sun." Sanguine Rose pointed to the sky. "Look! I told you we are going the right way! The sun is to our right. That's West. So, we've been heading south. The Hotel was south, right?"

"No." Liv put her head in her hands, defeated. "The Hotel was north. Oh my god... We're gonna die out here... Fuck this!"

"Keep your head up, Liv!"

"I'd like to change my first wish." Liv said, standing. "I wish for food. I am fucking starving. If a snake trap doesn't kill me, hunger will."

"Well why didn't you say so! You're in luck." Sanguine Rose said digging through her bag. "I always bring snacks." She pulled out brownies, smushed grapes and ketchup packets. She unwrapped a brownie and ate it, handing another to Liv. "Here. Brownies. And I have Girl Scout cookies here somewhere too. I'm a sucker for tagalongs."

Liv took one, sticky and half melted. "They're not like pot brownies or anything right? I mean, I would... but not in this situation. That would be a terrible high."

"No silly! They're just regular brownies. I gave the mushroom ones to the Bride-to-be. She was so excited!"

Liv ate the brownie in one bite. They were a little stale and dank. She contemplated the smushed grapes and ketchup packets. They didn't look half bad. "What do you think they're up to right now? The bachelorette party."

"Well... they're probably having fun. Like us!"

"Yeah, right..."

The party boat was full speed ahead back to the resort. The mood had soured like a stale sour patch kid forgotten under a couch cushion. All of them in the bachelorette party had too much sun and too little fun. Sobriety was fast coming and the hangover was hammering harder. Andre threw back another drink down his gullet. He had to keep that buzz going somehow. "These brownies ain't doing shit! Sanguine Rose is a has been!"

"Duds." Emily A shrugged.

"How much longer in this fucking boat?" Heather was pissed.

"We booked until sundown." Meadow said.

The Bride forced a smile. "Trust me girlies. It will be the best sunset you'll ever see." Then she puked off the side of the boat again, painting it yellow. Her skin was yellow, melty, wounds leaking pus covered in chalky makeup. The group did their best not to vomit themselves looking at her decay.

Back in the jungle Liv and Sanguine Rose were walking about. The sun was setting and the sky burned red. Liv giggled a bit, not knowing if it was the heat or the lack of water or maybe something else. "Sanguine Rose." She said and repeated. "Sanguine Rose. What a funny name!"

"You like it?"

"I love it. How'd you get it? Where were your parents from?"

"My parents are from New Jersey."

"No, I mean the name. Is it foreign?"

"Oh! Well, it's a Daedric item from Skyrim."

"The video game?"

"Yea. You play?"

"No... But my boyfriend... my ex. He did."

Sanguine Rose smiled. "I've spent way too many hours playing that game. My name is Rosemary. That's my real name. I just loved Skyrim so Sanguine Rose stuck."

"Real name." Liv laughed. "Rose... Mary." And she went full-blown goofy.

"Well, it looks like you're feeling better."

"I'm feeling really, really good actually."

"Yeah, me too." Sanguine Rose froze, eyes wide shut like that movie. She dug and dug through her bag. "Wait... wait. Oh fuck."

"Wait. Weight. Waight." Liv laughed loved so loud that the Yucatán Cartel could hear her from a half mile away. The Cartel followed the noise.

"Oh shit." Sanguine Rose whispered.

Liv kept laughing. "What is it babe?"

"I think I had a mix-up." The realization hit Sanguine Rose like a brick of cocaine.

"Mix up of what?"

"Those brownies... I was high before but now.... I'm like... really wavy... How are you feeling sweetheart? How high are you?"

"Hi, how are you?" Liv laughed love so hard she should be locked up. "How high are you! How high are you!"

The party boat pulled up to the resort dock, and that group of silver spooned scoundrels touched dry land. They were all pissed, seasick and sunburnt. And worst of all sober!

"Well, that was a buzzkill." Andre spit. "Fuck me. Those brownies were shit."

Becky shrugged and got off the boat as it docked. "Well snorkeling was fun. "

Meadow did a sloppy drunk headcount, then counted again. "Wait. Hold on girls. I'm a little tipsy but." She counted again.

"We're missing Emily." Heather said.

"I'm right here." Emily A waved.

"No not you Emily!" Meadow was livid. "The other Emily! Emily B!"

"Emily!" The Bride gasped. "Oh my god! Oh my god!"

"We have to go back!" Heather demanded the captain.

"This trip is cursed!" The Bride sobbed. "My bachelorette party is ruined!"

Meadow put on an act for her Bride-to-be. "No! It's not ruined! No. No. Don't say that. We still have dinner. And clubbing all black blackout. It's all gonna be ok. Right captain? It's gonna be ok?"

"We need to go back now and search for her." Bart was livid.

"You can surely find her... Right captain?" Meadow asked.

"She's fine." The captain scratched his beard. "This happens all the time."

"This happens all the time?" The Bride was livid as livid can be. "You lose girls all the time? What kind of captain are you? What kind of shit hole service is this?"

"Listen." The captain went on. "That cove is full of party boats. People get drunk and swim off to other party boats all the time. It happens. We'll go back and do another pass and look for her, but I wouldn't worry. She probably hitched a ride with another party. For all we know she's back at your hotel passed out in bed."

"Emily doesn't ditch." Emily A crossed her arms. "She's no ditcher!"

"You call yourself a professional?" Heather sneered at the captain. "How could you let this happen, cap'n?"

"This is so not cool." Bart shook his head. "We need to go back. Now."

Andre and Tanya exchanged a look like... really? For Emily B? Fuck it.

"Captain... are you sure she's on another boat... or got back safely?" Meadow asked.

"Almost positive." The captain sighed as his crew cleaned up the bachelorettes mess. "But we'll go back and do another pass and look for her."

"You see sweetie?" Meadow smiled big at the Bride. Too big, too fake. "Nothing to worry about!" The group was stunned, shocked, sunburnt and sobered up.

XXVI

FROLIC TIME

Liv and Sanguine Rose frolicked through the jungle in the fading light. The two of them were hand in hand jumping over downed trees. Through a dusky dreamy forest, the two pranced and danced like it was show time. The energy was quickly fading from Sanguine Rose, but Liv kept it up. She had as much energy as a teen at a house party after raiding her daddy's liquor cabinet.

"You know, this is fun and all," Sanguine Rose stopped to catch her breath, "but it's getting dark. We should stop and rest."

Liv twirled once, twice, and another time doing a 1080 spin if my math is correct. Dirt and sweat kicked up her bare ankles and thighs. "Now you want to stop?" She laughed. "But we're just getting started!"

"Come here, honey." Sanguine Rose pulled out a canteen of water. "Have some water."

Liv drank like she had never had water before. It was so fucking good, so refreshing. On the ground creepy crawly bugs crawled everywhere churning up the dirt with their slick thoraxed antennaed bodies. Liv avoided a bug and kicked something hard and cold. She bent down rubbing bugs off of its metal, rubbing it like a genie's lamp.

"Look!" She shouted. "It's a fucking gun! That's crazy." And sure enough lying there glistening in the moonlight was an assault rifle. It lay there like it was left on purpose. She bent down to inspect it.

Sanguine Rose heard voices in the jungle. Not friendly ones. It was the Yucatán Cartel. "Liv." She whispered. "Stay quiet. There's people out there."

Liv didn't hear. She was rubbing the gun like a drunk sailor and that's when her upside down turned to a frown and she grabbed her silly belly. "Hold on. Sanguine Rose. I'd like to tell you something. I really want to tell you something. Something I haven't told anyone."

"Maybe later."

Liv grabbed the gun and lifted it up. SNAP! A wire activated a booby trap above them. Two massive logs came down with enough force to crush a tank. They slammed together inches above Liv's soft head. It would have been her funeral had it not been for Sanguine Rose.

"Liv!" Sanguine Rose jumped at her, grabbed her. Together they fell through brush and over a hill, rolling down and down cradling each other, dirt in their mouths, bugs in their hair.

"Holy shit!" Liv screamed. The rifle was between them, safety off, the trigger activated. Shots rang out across the jungle.

The Yucatán Cartel men saw tracer rounds flying above the trees. They took cover. Liv and Sanguine Rose landed in a heap of moss and sat up covered in mud. They looked like they had crawled out of a dump truck. "Holy shit, this fucker is loaded." Liv laughed.

"Yeah, no shit." Sanguine Rose was out of breath. The Cartel was closing in. "I think we're gonna need it." She took the rifle and pulled Liv to her feet.

XXVII

DINNER IN HELL

That night the girls sat around a dinner table at a Spanish fusion restaurant called 'Holy Frijoles!' They looked like survivors of a plague. No one talked. No one smiled.

"Is no one going to say it?" Andre broke the silence first with the obvious. "Alright bitches, I will. We're cursed!"

Meadow waved for him to keep it down. The waiter approached the table, fake smile. "Does anyone have any allergies?" He asked.

"Yeah, I'm allergic to shellfish." Tanya raised her hand.

"First Brazil, now Emily." Emily A stirred her water.

"And where is Liv?" Becky asked.

"I'm really starting to get worried," said Bart.

"And that Sanguine Rose character. She's still missing." Tanya coughed..

"Everyone quiet... here she comes," Heather lowered her voice.

The Bride entered like death in high heels. She wore caked on makeup but couldn't hide her melty toxic damage. Her eyes were swollen from old tears and bubonic tonic.

The waiter head to the kitchen to grab another order of food. "Heads up," He got the chef's attention. "A girl out there has a shellfish allergy."

"Alright. No problem." The chef shrugged and pulled shrimp out of a boiling paella, like that would make a difference.

In the dark damp hot jungle, The Yucatán cartel came upon where Liv and Sanguine Rose had been, now gone. Nothing but footprints and bullet casings remained.

Nearby, Sanguine Rose tried to comfort Liv, who was tripping harder than she had ever tripped in her life. In her third eye, bugs the size of rats were crawling all over her body, slick and slimy and creepy crawly. In reality there was nothing more than a few mosquitos here and there, but to her third eye it was like that scene in Temple of Doom with all the bugs, you know the one I'm talking about. And if you don't know it look it up. It's at the 55-minute mark of the movie. But don't look it up now, do it later. Keep reading.

"Get them off!" Liv screamed.

"Quiet!" Sanguine Rose placed a hand over Liv's mouth. Too Late. The Cartel soldiers were right behind them!

Liv grabbed the automatic rifle from Sanguine Rose, safety off, and unloaded hell at the imaginary insects. To her it was like playing a video game, colorful and deadly. "Die motherfuckers!" Sanguine Rose covered her ears. "Get some!" Liv kept firing, hit a claymore near the Cartel. The claymore detonated BOOM! Setting off others like dominoes. BOOM! BLAM! KABLOOEY! The cartel hit the dirt, shrapnel flying over the heads of the lucky ones. The not so lucky ones were getting decapitated or getting slaughtered by their own traps and explosives.

"Retreat!" Marco of the Yucatán Cartel screamed. Too late for him. Marco ran right into a snake pit. He was ripped to pieces by hungry vipers. His jugular was torn out by nasty fangs. Blood, so much blood, like a lot of blood spurt out and pooled all around him painting him and the snakes red. Slick, he rolled around and around with the snakes over and over again painting them all redder and redder.

A server plated spaghetti with marinara. Dinner was served. Tanya dug into her paella (shrimp free thanks to the chef) like it was her last meal. News flash: It was. "Wow!" She exclaimed. "This is so good, like nothing I've ever had." Andre was at the bar talking to some cute bro who will come back later on in this story at a deadly game of golf.

At the head of the table the Bride held back her tears. Nothing would satisfy her, and all of her dreams of a perfect bachelorette party were collapsing all around. Meadow leaned in close and whispered to her. "Are you alright, sweetie? Can I get you a refill?"

"Everyone is ditching!" The Bride had the demeanor of a cranky toddler. "Am I not enough? Brazil gets fucking blown up! Sanguine Rose and Liv just fuck off to God knows where. Emily? She just ditched! Got on another party boat. Like, what the fuck? Am I not enough?" She was sobbing.

"Oh my god." Bart slammed his fork down. "Am I hearing you right? No one ditched you bitch."

"Whose side are you on!?" The Bride stood sulking, eyes red, face melty and greenish-yellow. Her head met her hands and she fucked off crying.

"Go on after her." Meadow nudged Heather. "I'll take care of the bill."

Heather hobbled after the bride. Tanya coughed, scratching her throat.

"You feeling alright?" Becky asked her.

"Yea... I just need some air." Tanya stumbled out of the restaurant coughing. Soon she found herself by some fountains and a man-made waterfall. No one seemed to care as her throat closed up tighter than a boa constrictor. She waved frantically for anyone who could help, the Bride, Heather, no one noticed, no one cared. And why would they? They had more important things going on anyway.

Tanya grabbed for her purse, searched for an EpiPen, found it, fumbled it, dropped it down the waterfall. She jumped after it, falling down the waterfall like a bad joke. Smashed her head on rocks, out cold. Dead. Goodbye Tanya.

XXVIII

QUINTANA ROO PLANNERS

"Miguel." Boss Antonio paced back and forth smoking an obnoxiously large cigar. "What did you discover?"

"I met the most beautiful girl." Miguel smiled. He was in love. "An American flower named Becky."

"What? No, you idiot. About the CIA! Anything at the hotel?"

"Oh, sorry boss. I have a lot on my mind. No operatives at the hotel boss. And that poison at the club the other night? It turns out it came from the Yucatán Cartel. They had a hitman disguised as a waiter. He slipped it in our drinks."

"Ouch!" Boss Antonio burnt his fingers with cigar ember. He tossed the cigar to the floor like it was an ex-girlfriend, grabbed a new cigar from his pack and lit it smoking in deep. "The Yucatán are dead men! We go to war!"

The morning sun crept up over the ocean illuminating the resort. Tanya's corpse bobbed in the waterfall pool like bloated garbage. It crashed over and over and over again into the rocks. Another bone snapped in a meat-bag of fast decaying flesh. No one would discover her body for another week at least. By that time her remains would be like wet paper towel wrapped around chicken bones.

Morning in the Jungle. Liv and Sanguine Rose were covered in mud like war paint. Their clothes were ripped and knotted. They looked like Amazon warriors. The morning sun cut rays through the damp air. "East. We head East," Sanguine

Rose directed. "We head to the water. We might be lost, but I'm sober now, I think. And that counts for something, right Liv?"

"Oh sure." Liv laughed like a broken thing needing fixing. She still cradled the rifle, empty of rounds now.

"You still feeling it?" Sanguine Rose asked her.

"I see things a bit differently today," Liv's eyes went from the woods to Sanguine Rose. She couldn't keep her center, her eyes kept drifting and darting. "Last night I wanted to tell you something. Didn't get the chance. It's something I haven't told anyone yet. But I want to tell you."

"Okay." Sanguine Rose said. "I'm glad you feel comfortable enough with me."

"I had an abortion this week." Liv didn't mince words. "There I said it. It was right before this trip. No one knows except my ex. And now you."

Sanguine Rose got down low and held Liv in her arms, pulled her close and whispered. "You are strength." And in that moment that was all Liv needed to hear.

Rustling, the Yucatán cartel was just beyond the trees. Boss Francisco led his troop. "Strength." Boss Francisco reminded his troop. "Marco was weak. I am your strength and strength is everything!"

"Boss can we-"

Boss Francisco didn't let his soldier finish, he grabbed him by the throat and threw him to the ground. "Shut up! Stay quiet! Do as I say!" Another soldier picked up his fallen comrade. No one liked Boss Francisco. No one trusted him.

Sanguine Rose shoved Liv against a dead tree, it swayed and decayed. "Stay quiet." She looked down at the gun. "How many rounds do you have left?"

"It's empty I think."

"Ah fuck-"

"Hello out there!" Boss Francisco called at the girls, held up his rifle, his troops followed him with hesitation. "Anyone out there?" Cartel guns locked and loaded.

"Are we going to die?" Liv asked Sanguine Rose. The tree they leaned against rocked back and forth, uneasy. It was as unsure of itself as they were. It had died many years ago and many living things had eaten right through it. And today that tree would meet its true destiny in the story of the Bloodbath Bachelorette.

"Whatever happens... have strength." Sanguine Rose reassured Liv. "Be brave." The tree cracked and teetered.

"I've got a bad feeling about this." A soldier complained whispering to another. He looked down the sights of his gun and aimed it all around then lowered his weapon. "We should turn back now."

"Keep your weapons up men!" Boss Francisco bossed them around.

They were so close now Liv could smell their stanking body odor. The Yucatán were just behind the dead tree. Liv leaned back hard and the dead tree cracked like thunder, fell like judgment. The girls fell with it. Francisco didn't even scream, he just looked up at his own demise. The tree crushed him like an overripe melon.

Dust was everywhere. Blood was everywhere. Liv rose up like a queen of the jungle in the dust. Sunlight hit her like a spotlight. It was her moment to shine. The Cartel forgot about their dead boss. They were in total shock and awe and pomp and circumstance of the beauty and power of Liv, queen of the jungle.

Sanguine Rose took advantage of the moment. "Behold your salvation!" She yelled out in perfect Spanish.

The Yucatán soldiers were stunned. They didn't know what to do or say. One of them began to tear up and slow clap and others followed. "The asshole Francisco is dead!" A soldier cheered. "Behold our new salvation!"

"Liv!" Sanguine Rose held her up.

"Behold our new salvation." Another Yucatán cheered and the rest all joined in cheering for their new leader: Liv. "All hail Liv! The wicked witch is dead!"

XXIX

FLESH AND CHROME

The morning was grim and gloomy for the bachelorette party. No one wanted to talk. No one wanted to celebrate. No one, definitely no one wanted to go to the scheduled pole dancing class at the resort gym. But it was Meadow's job to get the party's ass in gear. She rounded them all up like cattle to the slaughter and made sure they had a healthy breakfast. She waltzed them merrily to the dance studio at the resort gym in the building next to the other building next to the lobby. Wood flooring, mirrored walls, but I don't need to tell you, you've seen a dance studio before... Haven't you?

The bachelorette 'party' were dressed up in their gross animal print apparel. Disgusting. Bart thought maybe he should switch to black to match the theme of this funeral procession. Liv was ahead of the curve on this trip. She was a real trendsetter.

The pole instructor was all muscle and sweat and fake enthusiasm. He had a pencil-thin mustache like John Waters. "Alright ladies," he danced. "Like this!" He flipped upside down and all around, legs scissored. An impossible move for anyone who wasn't a wormy worm like he was.

"Where's Andre?" Heather asked Emily A leaning in.

"And where's Tanya?" Emily A asked her.

"Don't say it!" Meadow hissed like the snakey snake she was.

"That's right! " The Bride ugly laughed. She knew what was up. "You're all thinking it. I'm saying it. They ditched my party like everybody else!"

"No..." Bart spoke. "Don't you get it yet honey?"

"Get wha,t Bart?" The Bride flipped her hair and decayed flesh and bits and bobs came off with it. "Get what?"

"No one is ditching you." Bart stood up. He was the one-eyed man in the land of the blind. King.

"That takes years and years of practice my mademoiselles." The pole instructor finished showing off and took a bow. "But I'll start you girls off with something simpler."

"Oh, come on that looked easy." Alexa, drunk and cocky grabbed a pole. "Like this?"

"No honey! Not without a spotter!" The instructor lunged after her, but it was too late. Alexa flipped, slipped, and slid down the pole screaming. Her head hit the wood floor and her neck snap-crackle-popped on impact. "Jesus Christ!" The instructor was livid and horrified. Everyone was screaming.

"Sorry I'm late ladies." Andre walked in late as usual, Bluetooth headphones on to block out the screams. Then he saw her. "Holy shit!" He screamed.

"Nobody touch her!" Bart ran to Alexa before anyone else did. "Someone call 911!" Alexa's head was 180 degrees in the wrong direction. She was choking and coughing up blood and bile. It was not sexy. Alexa convulsed then went numb.

"Your friends aren't ditching you!" Bart screamed at the Bride and took Alexa's pulse. Alexa was dead as a doornail. There was fire in Bart's eyes. "Your friends are dying left and right!"

"Liv and Sanguine Rose are probably still fine though, right?" Becky asked.

Liv and Sanguine Rose were in the jungle hot with blood and fire. They had shed their old selves. What remained or rather what emerged were their true selves. They were fresh-faced warlords. They were feral. They were focused. They were unrelenting. Directing their new Yucatán army, they carved out ambush points with military precision. They hovered over maps and compasses stained with mud and blood. They pointed, planned and smiled. The Yucatán watched and learned.

On Liv and Sanguine Rose's instruction, the Yucatán rebuilt their old booby traps. Sanguine Rose dipped her finger into the cartel's cocaine stash like she was sampling a tasty pie. She snooted, then put the leftovers in her gums. Yummy. Thumbs up from the Yucatáns. Thumbs up from Sanguine Rose. The Yucatáns were impressed. Orders weren't barked at by Liv and Sanguine Rose, they were given and understood. Liv and Sanguine Rose were part of the team. The Yucatán was awake again. They were alive under new management.

Overhead the sky was churning, black clouds gathering like a bad omen. Rolling in slow and heavy and dark. The jungle didn't move, it waited in anticipation. A storm was coming. The Quintana Roo would attack at dusk.

XXX

SPA DAY

Becky and Emily A strolled into the Resort Spa like they owned the place. The decorations were over the top, Aztec meets Roman baths. Gross. Nothing made sense and why would it? A receptionist named Dolores sat at the reception desk greeted the two bimbos. Dolores was so bored with her job she might as well have been embalmed. "Welcome to the resort spa." She greeted them like a funeral director about to show off their urn options. "Do you have a reservation?"

"Yes, hi." Emily A smiled a fake fucking smile. "For Becky and Emily."

Dolores flipped through an oversized appointment book like it was 1983. Nearby, two jaded electricians stood over a busted electrical panel and argued about which was better, 120v or 127v or the UK's 230v or who knows, really? I don't, and neither did they. I'm not a Mexican electrician but maybe you are so you would know better.

"Nothing in this place works!" One electrician complained to the other.

"Lunch?" The other suggested.

"Sounds good." And they clocked out leaving a mess of wires and tools behind. Uh-oh.

"Ah yes. Couples massage..." Dolores found the page with their reservation. "You were scheduled for tomorrow with a group but-"

"Things changed!" Emily A snapped. "We are here now-" she took a deep breath and changed her tone. "And we are in desperate need of relaxation."

"Well, our masseuses are all booked up." Dolores nodded. "But the wellness spa is open. We have steam rooms, saunas, whirlpools-"

"Say less." Emily A was so rude these days. "I have to sweat out this hangover."

"Very well. This way please." Dolores glided over the floors and led the ladies to the locker room. The lockers were grand and many, and the girls found comfort in fresh robes and slick sandals, quickly undressing and wrapping themselves in plush fabric.

The sauna was large enough to fit and terminate 20 souls comfortably. Inside were rows of wooden benches and in the center an electric furnace. Emily A yanked open the heavy wooden door to the sauna and walked in like she was home.

"This is exactly what I needed!" Emily A exclaimed. "Becky, turn it to max."

"What?"

"The Heat! Max it out! Turn this thing up!"

Becky cranked up a dial on the heater past 11.

"Ah yes." Emily sat cozy, the furnace's coals turned from red to orange, heavy heat radiating off of them. "Exactly what I needed. Just sweat it out."

Becky fidgeted. Ten sweltering minutes passed like an eternity in that heat. Becky wiped sweat off her brow and off her ass crack. "That's enough for me." She got up and struggled to open that heavy wooden door. With a heavy grunt it groaned open. "Alright, see you later Emily." When the door slammed shut its wooden handle bent backwards, stuck forever, sealing Emily in her sweltering wooden tomb.

The Sauna was cranking overtime. Outside an electrical box was on the fritz, hot coiled metal melting cheap plastic. The coals in the sauna turned from orange to yellow and yellow to white hot! Emily sat up boiling, disoriented. Her face was lobster red. "I'm cooked!" The air was thick with heat waves. She stood dizzy, stumbled and fell right onto the hot coals screaming! Her towel ignited first, then her skin boiled, cracked, peeled. She clawed at the door banging with bloody blackened fists as the sauna combusted all around her. Flames licked up its wooden walls, smoke thick as storm clouds. No one heard her pleas for help. No one heard her banging. She was trapped in a burning coffin. And after a few terrifying minutes that was the end for Emily A.

Black smoke rolled thick from the roof of the Spa building and out into the hot Tulum sky. The Bride, Heather and Meadow didn't seem to notice or care. They figured it was coming from the resort grill. Smelled nice. They gunned for the hotel lobby. "We have lunch next." Meadow scrolled through the itinerary on her phone. "Yum, something smells good, must be a barbecue."

"I can't eat." The Bride itched at her infection.

"Then might I suggest the beach?" Meadow suggested. "Tanning!"

"It looks like rain." Dark clouds were forming overhead and the black smoke from the sauna fire met the sky.

Meadow refused defeat. "Fine, no lunch, no beach. Let's just head back to your room and get ready for the concert! Do a little pregame before Bad Bunny! Get excited!"

"Yea, I guess." The Bride was depressed. "Where'd Emily and Becky go? And Andre?"

"Um-" Heather answered nervously. "Emily and Becky went to the spa."

"Dummies!" Meadow clapped and fake laughed. "Spa day is tomorrow! They went a day early!"

"They ditched like everyone else." The Bride was bitter.

"No." Meadow kept up the lie to save face. "They're just dumb!"

Andre walked past the group trying his best to hide himself from the girls. He carried shopping bags full of golf attire and accessories.

"Ooh there's Andre!" Heather called out.

Andre was busted. He smiled sheepish to the ladies. "Oh, hi ladies." He hid his shopping bags as best he could.

"What are you up to Andre?" Meadow asked his hungover ass.

"Yea, and what's with all the golf stuff?" The Bride poked.

"We're gonna get ready and pregame, want to join us?" Meadow asked with a fake smile.

"I can't. I have a date." Andre answered bashful but proud.

"Slay Andre!" Heather cheered but then changed her tone when she saw Meadow and the Bride's expression of downright disapproval. "Wait... Not cool Andre. You should come pregame with us instead! Invite your date!"

"Are you fucking kidding me Andre?" The Bride was pissed.

"You're going on a date?" Meadow always had the Bride's back. "Right now? After all of this? You need to cancel."

"Listen... it's been fun and all." Andre shrugged. "Actually, you know what? No. It hasn't been fun at all. This is my vacation too you know! My job only gives me two weeks off every year. I have to make it count."

"Does that include holidays?" Heather asked dumbly.

"I'm out." Andre swung his bag around and a pair of socks flew out and hit Meadow squarely in the face. The Bride shrugged her shoulders in furious disappointment and beelined for the lobby bar. Meadow scurried after her, and Heather hobbled on after the both of them like would be roadkill.

Outside of the spa Becky meandered, lightheaded from the heat. She dug through her purse and found Sanguine Rose's valet ticket. Heavy smoke rose off the Spa building. A fire engine pulled up to the curb, siren blaring, tires screeching. Firefighters jumped out, connected a hose line to a hydrant, ran past Becky to the Spa with a charged hose in hand. Becky turned back to check out the firefighters' firm buttocks. Sexy. She completely neglected the burning building. In an instant she collided with Miguel of the Quintana Roo Cartel who just so happened to be walking in the opposite direction as her.

"I'm so sorry, Becky." Miguel said with words like silk.

"I'm so sorry, Miguel. We can't keep bumping into each other like this." Becky was breathing hot and heavy.

"There is no one else I'd rather bump into than you. Are you alright? We really collided there."

"Your muscles." Becky caressed his arms. "So firm and strong."

Miguel massaged Becky's shoulder. She grabbed both of his strong arms and leaned up for a kiss. At first Miguel was in shock but then he melted away in her soft embrace. They closed their eyes and kissed in utter romance. It was like a soap opera finale. Becky broke away and giggled.

"What is so funny, mi amor?" He asked her.

"I just wish I'd done that sooner. I leave tomorrow." Becky sighed, massaging his strong arms.

"You are the sun and the stars, my Becky! Miss your flight. Be with me."

"Oh, Miguel."

"Oh, Becky!"

They stood there locked in a passionate kiss as firefighters rushed past them on either side. The building burned behind them bathing them in orange light. There was a clap of distant thunder and smoke on the horizon.

XXXI

𝒯ORE!

The sky was rotting, sickly gray and green. A distant flash of lightning and the wind picked up like a vendetta. Andre and his cute date, Johnny Boy, teed off at the resort's golf course. Andre was dressed like a walking ad for a golf shop, plaid shorts, pastel polo, stupid visor. His shorts still had the tags on it. He clumsily grabbed for a club. He had no clue what he was doing but Johnny Boy was confident as hell. He already had his ball on the tee, driver in hand.

"So, Johnny Boy," Andre asked smirking. "You think it's okay to play in this weather?" There was a Soft rolling thunder.

Johnny Boy took his swing. Whack! A beautiful shot straight down the center. "This storm? This is nothing! Come on." He unzipped a fanny pack and took out two little tequila shooters. "Care for a nip sip?" They clinked plastic and downed the booze. Andre approached the tee clueless.

"How hard can this be?" Andre asked himself.

"Keep your head down." Johnny Boy instructed. "Eyes on the ball."

Andre grinned. "If this date goes well, I'm gonna have my eye on your balls. Balls deep." He swung, sliced. The golf ball dropped into the jungle like a limp dick. "Fuck me!"

"If you say so," Johnny Boy laughed. "Let's call it a mulligan!"

Andre kept at it again and again, locating his ball and sliced through grass like he was trying to kill the golf course. All the while the sky grew darker, and the thunder grew louder.

Andre churned up more grass and dirt with his club than a farmer did plowing a field. It was a massacre. All around them were potential hazards, potential ways to kill themselves: Exposed wiring, cracked glass, stray metal that could kill. How would Andre meet his bitter end?

A foursome of players waited behind the couple quietly judging. Andre was on the green now. His ball landed two feet from the hole. He putted and missed. "Wow. I suck."

"We'll see about that." Johnny Boy tapped the ball in for him. Lightning split the sky and the rain arrived, soft at first.

"Jesus!" Andre was so startled he nearly pissed himself.

"Talk about timing!" Johnny Boy laughed. "Only seventeen more holes to go." The foursome gave up and called it a day with the incoming weather.

"That was only one hole?" Andre couldn't believe it.

"Come on cutie, let's keep moving." Johnny Boy headed to their golf cart.

Andre threw his clubs into the back of their golf cart and climbed in. Johnny Boy gunned it like they were in a race. "You know," Andre rubbed Johnny Boy's firm thigh. "All this sports stuff is fun and all, but we can find a couple more holes to play with back in my room." He was as smooth as stained velvet and as a convincing as a naughty gay car salesman.

Johnny Boy took Andre's hand and moved it higher and higher until it rested on top of his firm package. "Would you feel this right here?"

Andre did enthusiastically. Too enthusiastically. Johnny Boy closed his eyes in bliss, missed the path. The golf cart veered off course, straight onto the green.

"Fore!" Another golfer screamed teeing off.

Lightning struck and the ball came flying at the couple like a missile, smacking Andre in the mouth. His teeth exploded like popcorn. Blood sprayed. Andre slammed forward into the cart's steering wheel, painful gurgling, swallowing enamel and blood. Johnny Boy lost control, launched over a ravine and into a boggy pond. Splish splash crash! The cart rolled and flipped upside down in the water. Andre plunged into the muddy bog. Underwater, trapped under the cart, choking, gasping, swallowing bog water, blood, turf and mud. His lungs filled to the brim with mud, drowning him. Above him the cart settled in the muck like a tombstone. Johnny Boy managed to escape and fled the scene still fully erect. The sky opened up and flash flood. Andre's waving hand was the last we saw of him. It went limp and fell into the muck. And that was the end for Andre.

XXXII

JUNGLE WARFARE

The army of the Quintana Roo Cartel came at dusk for the Yucatán. The jungle rains turned from drizzle to deluge. The sky cracked. Lightning went up like white trees in the clouds. Each crack of light revealed wet soldiers in the dark jungle. Rifles, helmets, grenades, fierce eyes, gnawing teeth. Liv and Sanguine Rose led the Yucatán cartel from behind a heavy machine gun. The Yucatán soldiers, faces painted, hearts thumping. They screamed war cries.

Who fired the first shot no one could say for certain, but once one fired, they all fired in the unfolding bedlam. Gunfire snapped through the trees, bullets ripped through wood and men alike. Bloody murder and shrill screaming. The air was filled with panic and gun smoke.

Sanguine Rose fed the ammo belt into the heavy machine gun and Liv fired. Rat-a-tat-tat. Bones shattered and limbs flew. Booby traps went off like planned. Exploding claymores, tripwires, snake pits and spike pits. The Quintana Roo soldier's death rattle screams turned primal. A cartel truck exploded, someone caught fire and fell burning into a snake pit. The rains kept coming, fresh blood and piss running away to the many streams and rivers.

The Quintana Roo Army never had a chance. They were on Yucatán turf. It wasn't long before the last Quintana Roo soldier took his last breath. The Yucatán held their fire. Only the sounds of the rain remained, steam rose off the heat of the bodies and twisted metal.

Liv breathed heavy, fingers curled on the trigger. Sanguine Rose had no more ammo to feed her. She wiped blood from her cheek. The Yucatán screamed for victory and lifted up Sanguine Rose and Liv in celebration. They paraded them around the camp, mud slick, faces painted, battle-worn little demons. They were victorious.

Miles away, Boss Antonio smoked a fat cigar in the safety of his headquarters. He was seated at a large wooden table. On the table sat a loaded pistol and a silver plate of cocaine. His phone rang. He picked it up.

"You have an update for me?" Boss Antonio asked.

"It's no good boss," came the nervous voice on the phone. "They wiped us out."

"And Miguel?" Boss Antonio asked.

"No one can find him, boss."

Antonio hung up. He took a long drag of his cigar, rubbed his temples and placed a firm hand on his loaded pistol.

XXXIII

STRUTTING YOUR STUFF

Wind, sirens, rain like nails. The ocean churned black and bloated. Three trashed women moved like trash in a storm. It was the Bride, Heather and Meadow in gross yellow ponchos, all huddled under one useless clear umbrella. They walked to an empty stage. On barricades, signs read in big black letters: SHOW CANCELLED.

"You've got to be fucking kidding me!" The botulism Bride cried, tears mixed with rainwater and pus.

"Wow." Heather gave her two cents and that was all she had left to give. CRACK! Lightning struck. The useless umbrella twisted out of their hands like used toilet paper and flew straight into the ocean to commit suicide. It had the right idea.

"It's over." The Bride turned crying. "Let's go back inside."

But Meadow? Meadow was possessed to party. "It's not over!" She shouted, eyes wide, hair soaked and expression plastered. "It's happening. We're here. We've got this. Right Heather?" She sprinted to the stage, climbed up, one leg in a puddle, the other twirling over a speaker cable. Almost ate it, didn't care. It was time to dance! Arms out, laughing and tripping over herself intoxicated in emotional agony.

Heather kept in place, stayed on the beach with the Bride, wobbling, shivering, soggy, unsure. The Bride's mouth dropped. "What are you doing Meadow?!"

Rain came harder, a full monsoon. Meadow danced and yelled in it, not a care in the world. "Come on! What's your favorite Bad Bunny song? The one that always cheers you up?"

"Moscow Mule." The Bride didn't hesitate.

Meadow grinned like a lunatic. "I don't know that one, but remember this one?"

She belted out "Gasolina" by Daddy Yankee. Off key and too loud. She stomped across the stage, hair flipping, sparks popping under her dancing feet.

"That's Daddy Yankee," the Bride muttered, but Meadow didn't care to listen. She was strutting her stuff, like she was made of lightning. She grabbed a truss tower, dropped low like a stripper and popped back up standing tall and proud. CRACK! Lightning struck the stage. The whole place lit up like fireworks. Electrical current ran through Meadow's body, she was magnetized to the truss. Lightning went through her like an X-ray and for a moment you could see her skeleton like a Scooby Doo cartoon. Arms, ribs, jaw, every bone inside her fused together and glowed white.

All the stage lights exploded. Glass rained down like party confetti. It sliced Heather and the Bride on impact. Only a flesh wound. Shoulder, scalp, lips, bloody under their yellow ponchos. They all screamed, but nothing like Meadow's last scream. She screamed a blood-curdling scream as all the air escaped her lungs. Her skin peeled, ash and steam. Black curling skin coming off of her muscles like burnt paper. There was raw meat underneath. Muscle wired in blue and yellow arcing electricity. She combusted from the inside out then quite literally exploded. There was nothing left but blood and smoke.

All of it reflected in the Bride's wide horrified eyes. Blood running down her trembling lips. And that was the end for Meadow.

XXXIV

THE MAID OF HONOR LINE OF SUCCESSION

The rain had given up. The Yucatán soldiers looked out upon their victory still high on it. They cheered for the two queens that had handed them a win. Liv and Sanguine Rose were soaked in Quintana Roo Cartel blood. The two of them would be legends for years to come for the Yucatán. They were offered anything they wanted, and all they asked for was a ride home.

A Jeep rolled up, engine roaring. Liv and Sanguine Rose jumped in. "It's been a pleasure, boys!" Sanguine Rose waved them goodbye.

Liv slid further down in her seat. "Let's get the hell out of here." The Jeep peeled out, tires ripping up mud. The girls in the back like Yucatán royalty. No sirens, no speeches, and no guilt.

The storm had given up. Just seafoam riding up the sand. In the dark Heather and the Bride held onto each other like they were the last two people on Earth. Bloody cuts all over them, eyes swollen. "Are we next?" The Bride cried. "Are we going to fucking die?"

"No." Heather lied. "It's all going to be okay, girly. I got you." But both of them knew that wasn't true. They were soaked and shaking and stranded in a hell on earth that they had been told and sold would be week in paradise.

"We're so lost," The Bride cried. "Where even are we?"

Heather pointed, hobbling forward. "This way. The lobby is this way." The Bride stopped in her stumbling tracks, embraced Heather like it meant something. "Come on, we'll get pneumonia if we stay out here." Heather complained.

Like a joke with no punchline the Bride started up. "Heather, you are so amazing. You are really one of a kind. I love you. Under all of the current circumstances I think it's only right I ask you. Would you do me the honor being my new maid of honor?"

Heather gasped like it was the best thing she'd heard in her whole cursed life. "Oh my God yes! I thought you'd never ask!"

"It was always meant to be you!" They hugged, wet bloody and clumsy. "This is destiny!" They exchanged blood and mascara mixed with the Bride's pus. A long awkward beat, just the sound of waves.

"Let's get inside." Heather suggested.

The Jeep carrying Liv and Sanguine Rose tore down a slick muddied road. The Yucatán Soldier driving stayed quiet, sunglasses on at night. Too cool for Tulum School. He turned onto a paved road covered in thick curling fog and floored it.

"The lobby is this way?" The Bride asked Heather ditching her to cross the foggy road.

"Wait for me!" Heather hobbled after her. Then headlights, fast and bright. Heather turned just in time to die. The Yucatán Jeep slammed through her like vengeance. Heather's body cracked in half, exploded like a 12-gauge shotgun firing through a honey dew melon. One half of her landed on one side of the road, and the other up in a tree. No last words, no scream, just dead meat. And that was the end of hobbling Heather.

The Bride watched it happen. Mouth open, hands shaking. Her new maid of honor was gone in a blink of an eye. The Jeep screeched to a stop. Liv and Sanguine Rose popped out of the car stunned at the carnage. Parts of Heather were stuck in the Jeep's grill. Parts of Heather fell out of a tree.

"Adios!" The Yucatán driver yelled, and the Jeep peeled out, leaving the girls in a fog of exhaust and shock.

The Bride blinked, "Liv?" She couldn't believe her eyes at the sight of the amazon garbed beauties. "Oh my God it is you! And Sanguine Rose!" She called out to them like it was a high school reunion in hell. "You guys showed up! Wait- what are you wearing? Did you go to a theme party without me? Ugh, whatever, you're both forgiven. I'm so happy you're here! We can still make the afters. It'd be great to party with my maid of honor! It's our last night!

Liv didn't smile. Didn't blink.

"Pack your shit," She was dead serious. "We're going home."

XXXV

THE END

Sunrise. Waves like breathing. Hotel beds unmade. Streets all empty except for a single car carrying two lovers. Becky and Miguel sped off in Sanguine Rose's Jeep. The two of them were enveloped in sweat, love and stolen torque. They had spent the night in deep passion. They had fucked until dawn. Becky had even stuck a finger up Miguel's butt and he liked it. He liked it a lot. They drove straight at the horizon. They drove toward their future together, whatever that meant and however long that would be.

The airport tarmac wasn't nearly as romantic. The final survivors of the bloodbath bachelorette dragged their swollen suitcases toward their soon departing plane. It was Liv, Bart, Sanguine Rose and the Bride. The sad sack remainders. All broken, all falling apart.

Bart climbed the airstairs to the plane first, then Liv, then Sanguine Rose. The Bride wouldn't climb, she stood pouting. She cracked and buried her face deep into her hands sobbing.

"Might as well go to her." Bart shrugged when Liv looked to him for advice.

Liv begrudgingly walked back down the air stairs, stepped carefully. "Come on," she tapped the Brides shoulder. "Let's go home."

"This is all your fault, Liv!" The Bride looked up, face melting, skin peeling, hands sticky with gunk and tears.

"My fault?"

"You are a fucking curse! The plane, the tray table, your goddamned suitcase. It all started with you! The lock on the bathroom door and then Brazil! You spread your curse like a cancer at my party."

Liv had nothing to say. She was repulsed, not just with the Bride's appearance but with who she had become. Or maybe she was always this way. There would be no redemption arc for the Bride. Some people can't change. Liv walked back up the air stairs. It was over.

The Bride backed up in shock, nearing a pothole, the same one from the beginning of this story if you remember. Nearby a prop plane coughed and spooled up its engines. "Nothing to say, Liv? Nothing to defend yourself?" The Bride spit pus and stumbled screaming over the engine noise. "I wasn't going to say anything, but you know what? I don't give a fuck anymore. I know Liv. I know about the whole thing. Yeah, that's right. Your ex called me last week. Wanted my advice. I told him to dump your ass. He told me about the abortion. Yeah, I know the whole fucking story!"

Liv stopped but refused to turn around and look at the Bride.

"You are a cantankerous curse! Meadow was right." The Bride kept backing up. "She's dead but she was right. You are the devil!"

The prop plane turned, propeller spinning fast. The Bride was walking right into the plane.

"You don't even have the balls to look at me when I'm talking to you!" The Bride spat.

Liv turned to face her old friend one last time. "Watch out!" Liv screamed in terror, but it was too late.

The Bride's heel twisted. Her foot was stuck in the pothole. The propeller was right at her. She looked up at it but it was too late. Propeller made impact, began grinding the back of her skull like a deli meat slicer. She was locked in place. Slice after mutilated slice and she was unable to free herself from her imminent demise. Her brain detached from her spine and was thrown up in the air. Blood spilled out of her mouth like a chocolate fountain. Her eye sockets empty, mouth agape now empty, light spilled from behind her eye sockets and then her face was torn off completely. Her body was sucked up and shredded in the propeller and thrown up and away. Liv watched in terror. Her face was covered in the Bride's blood. Eyes wide with nothing left to say. That's one way to end a party.

THE END